An Augathella Baby

ANNIE SEATON

Augathella Short and Sweets: 2

ISBN: 978-1-923048-12-6

AUGATHELLA SHORT AND SWEETS

An Augathella Surprise

An Augathella Baby

An Augathella Spring

An Augathella Wedding

An Augathella Winter

An Augathella Ball

An Augathella Christmas

Following on from:

THE AUGATHELLA GIRLS

Book 1: Outback Roads –The Nanny

Book 2: Outback Sky – The Pilot

Book 3: Outback Escape – The Sister

Book 4: Outback Winds – The Jillaroo

Book 5: Outback Dawn – The Visitor

Book 6: Outback Moonlight – The Rogue

Book 7: Outback Dust – The Drifter

Book 8: Outback Hope – The Farmer

CHAPTER 1

Sophie – Lara Waters

Sophie glanced across at Kent as she climbed out of bed. She inched out slowly, not wanting to wake him, even though her husband had said last night he'd have to have an early start today. He and Jon Ingram were off mustering at six-thirty.

It was still dark, but the moon shining through their large bedroom window highlighted Kent's face. Sophie stood beside the bed and looked down at him. Sound asleep and breathing evenly, his features appeared totally relaxed. He looked like the sixteen-year-old boy she'd fallen in love with, not the rugged cattleman of these days.

Despite his deep slumber, Sophie knew as soon as the alarm went off at five-thirty, Kent would spring out of bed full of energy and enthusiasm about the day ahead, no matter what he had planned. She adored this man; his constant positivity and happiness had made such a difference to her life.

Sophie's only regret was that they'd split up before they were engaged and she'd spent—no, she'd wasted—three years with Jock Evans, three years which she'd blocked from her memory.

Those years of emotional—and some physical—bullying by Jock, during the months after the accident that had killed Braden's wife, Julia, had been hard. Sophie had taken in her brother's three sons to mother because Braden's grief had consumed him. The regret that she had left Kent before all that had happened was always with her, but she knew she had grown into a stronger person from the choices she'd made. When Kent had accompanied Braden to

Innot Springs last year to rescue her from a difficult situation, Sophie had come to her senses.

Thank God, Kent had never stopped loving her, and she knew that he had always been the man for her. She had fallen for Jock's sister's malicious lies when she should have known to trust Kent.

Their wedding had been a joyous affair until the accident that had threatened her nephew Petie's life. He had recovered and they had set off on their delayed honeymoon in Fiji. In the months since then, their married life at Lara Waters station had been happy and fulfilling.

Sophie let out a soft sigh; only one thing made her a little less happy at times. Kent desperately wanted a baby. He was already talking about when they had boys like Braden's three—actually four boys and a girl now with the arrival of little Meg and Munro a couple of months ago. He was looking forward to their kids being old enough to get out on the motorbikes and four-wheelers. Sophie had managed to brush off his comments or just simply smile.

The truth was, she wasn't ready, and her big worry was that she never would be. It was not a conversation she wanted to have with Kent in the first year of their marriage, but it had given her some sleepless nights as he talked more and more about their future family.

Turning to the door, Sophie picked up her satin bathrobe and slipped it on. She'd had every intention of getting up early—five a.m. was perhaps a little bit early—but making the biscuits and being ready to deliver them to Jenna for her grand opening had meant getting out of bed before dawn.

Sophie yawned, quietly closed the bedroom door and padded barefoot to the kitchen. She and Kent had gotten hooked by a comedy series about soccer in England last night, and they'd binge-watched a whole season after dinner. Of course, it was midnight before they went to bed, on the one night they should have gone to bed early. She had the baking to do, and then helping Jenna with what she was sure would be a very busy day at the official opening of the Vintage Tea Shop on the highway. Kent was behind on the mustering. Luke Elliott, one of the managers from Dwyer Holdings, was flying up from Narrabri today to see if the cattle were ready.

As well as the huge workload managing the stock on their property entailed, Kent also managed a thousand head of cattle on the property adjacent to Lara Waters. The property was owned by the Narrabri company and was currently between managers. Kent and Luke had become good mates over the past months. Sophie enjoyed Luke's company too, and instead of staying in the staff dongas on his last couple of visits, they had hosted Luke in their home.

She filled the kettle and switched it on; a cup of coffee would get her moving. Another yawn overtook Sophie as she stood at the kitchen window looking out as the first rosy pink glow tinged the eastern horizon, gradually creeping across the dark of the night.

It looked like the weather promised to deliver a good day for Jenna's opening. The sky was clear, and the last stars of the night quickly faded as the sky lightened. She turned her head to the side as the lowing of a distressed beast drifted in through the open kitchen window. She'd have to tell Kent about that as soon as he appeared.

After a quick coffee, her tiredness and yawns gone, Sophie set to work and half an hour later when she heard the alarm go off in their bedroom, four trays of jam drops were cooking in the oven. Kent appeared in the doorway as she lifted two of the trays out of the combustion stove.

'Yum. Jam drops for breakfast.'

She glanced across at him and shook her head as he reached out for one. 'Nope. If you want jam drops, you have to come to the opening.'

'Spoilsport.' Kent reached for Sophie instead and pulled her into his arms. He smelled clean and fresh, and his hair was damp from the shower. 'Good morning, my darling. It was lonely waking up in an empty bed.'

Sophie looped her arms around his neck, and her fingers brushed the damp curls on Kent's neck as she looked up at him. 'You need a haircut. And the bed wasn't empty. You were in it.'

'But I didn't have a wife to cuddle.'

'I have to make dozens of biscuits. I promised Jenna. She's panicking that she hasn't got enough food for the opening this afternoon.' She reached up and pressed a kiss on his lips. 'Any chance at all of you getting there before it's over? Everyone's going to be there. Please, sweetie?'

'As much as I'd love to, Soph, I'm going to be too busy. It's the only day Jon could give me. I guess Fallon will be disappointed too.'

'She will. It can't be helped. I know Luke's coming through today.' Sophie hid her disappointment. 'That reminds me, I could hear a beast out there before. It sounds like it's in trouble.'

'Okay, a quick cup of tea and I'd better get out there. You know if we keep having these late nights and separate mornings, we're never going to get those babies made.' He pulled her back against him, and Sophie closed her eyes as Kent kissed her thoroughly.

The oven timer dinged, and Sophie pulled

away. She smiled as Kent poured hot water on top of half a dozen Weet-Bix. By the time he'd finished his cereal, Sophie had two trays of Anzacs baking and was mixing up a batch of Melting Moments. Quickly drinking his tea, Kent carried his plate and cup to the sink before looping his arms around her waist again. 'Have a lovely day, sweetie. I'm sorry I can't be there, but I promise if there's any way that I can get into town before three, I will. Okay?' He bent down, and his lips were warm against her neck. 'I'm sorry I can't come. You have a good time,' he said. 'Bring me home something nice to eat.'

Sophie softened, and she cupped his cheek with her hand. 'What would you like me to bring home?'

'Does Jenna have any vanilla slices?' he asked.

Sophie chuckled. 'Jenna makes the best vanilla slices ever. Not with SAOs but with real puff pastry. I've got to stop sampling all her cakes. My jeans are getting tight.'

'You still look beautiful to me.' He dropped another kiss on her cheek and her mood thawed a little. 'I must come into town as soon as I get these cattle sorted and sample all these cakes. And catch up with Reg. I haven't talked to him for ages. Oh, and while I think of it, Ben and Amelia are going to come over for a barbie one night next week. Ben and I have been invited to play at the Tambo pub the night of the show. We want to practise some new songs.'

'That would be nice. You just make a date with Ben, whatever suits them.' She raised her eyebrows. 'Then again, Ben and Amelia will probably be at the opening today. I can talk to them.'

'Don't put the guilts on me, love. I'd love to come, you know that.'

'I wasn't. I was just making an observation.'

She hid her annoyance. 'How about I help you with the cattle tomorrow?'

'Great. I have to go over and help Braden before the end of the week. Do you want to come with me?'

'That'd be good. Callie said she's right for a couple of days this week, but any opportunity to see Meg and Munro is one I'll take. Plus, I can help you and Braden with the cattle,' she added as an afterthought.

Kent's lips were warm as he kissed her goodbye. 'Drive safe, sweetie.' He picked up the tucker box he'd packed last night before they went to bed and turned to the door. Sophie crossed to the sink where the trays of biscuits were cooling. 'Hang on, I'll put some jam drops in your tucker box.' Kent was still smiling as he looked back at her when he walked out the back door.

CHAPTER 2

Kent - Lara Waters

Kent jumped on his motorbike and rode the kilometre to the front gate. He was on time but Jon wasn't there yet. He climbed off the bike and put it behind the large timber mailbox, securing it with the padlock and chain he carried. Times had changed so much since he was a kid. They'd never had to secure anything back in those days. Now you had to lock up the house when you went to town and make sure there were no keys left in the station vehicles.

He unlocked the mailbox in case one of his neighbours had left something there, but it was empty. Now that the postal service had cut back rural deliveries to outlying stations—Lara Waters wasn't far enough out of town to qualify for delivery by air—he or Sophie made sure they were in town at least a couple of times a week to pick up the mail. Now that Sophie was helping Jenna at the new shop on the highway near Augathella, he didn't have to go to town so often.

Kent grabbed his tucker box off the back of the bike, climbed up on the fence rail, and sat waiting for Jon to arrive. He could see the plume of dust from Jon's vehicle approaching, but he was still a couple of kilometres away. He was worried about Sophie; if he didn't know better, a man would think his wife was avoiding him, but he shook himself and reminded himself of the loving kiss Sophie had given him as he'd left.

But one thing he hadn't missed was the way she was avoiding talking about having kids. Whenever he mentioned it, she either just smiled or changed the subject. It didn't mean anything; maybe if he was honest and told her he had some worries, they could talk about it, but so far, the opportunity hadn't arisen. They were both settling into married life and had a lot to adjust to. Sophie was busy; she was helping Jenna at the tea rooms plus baking at home; she was also going across to Kilcoy Station two or three times a week to help Callie out with the twins, as well as going to town to pick the boys up from school twice a week.

Sometimes he wondered if she was keeping busy so she wasn't at home with him, but again, he knew that it was just Sophie being Sophie. She was a good person, and she pitched in and helped wherever help was needed. And to be honest, he'd been so late home over the past few weeks, she would have been home by herself anyway. He always had to push away the thought that they'd broken up once. And that made him all the more determined to be honest and tell her what he was worried about. Communication and talking things out together was the key.

Having to work today sent guilt spiralling

sky-high. If Luke hadn't been flying in, Kent would have taken the afternoon off and made sure he was at the opening. Jenna's Vintage Tea Room on the highway was the talk of the town, or rather the talk of the district. And Sophie was really enjoying helping out.

He had to learn to stop worrying and to trust; sharing his worries with her would lighten the load. He was so immersed in his thoughts he didn't even hear Jon pull up until he called out to him.

'You coming, mate?'

Kent jumped off the fence and climbed in. 'Gidday, mate. Thanks for collecting me.' He slammed the door of the work ute shut and Jon took off again.

'Sorry, I was a bit late. Ryan had a bad night. Teething, we think.'

'Bit young for that, isn't he? Not that I know anything about babies.' Kent reached over and put his tucker box behind the seat.

Jon yawned and nodded. 'According to Ruth, five months is normal. But honestly, mate, I can take the crying, the poor little mite; it's the nappies that are the worst. It's worse than calf scours.' Jon looked over and caught Kent's grin. He chuckled. 'I know. Whoever thought we'd be having this sort of conversation? Wait until it's your turn. I'll be the expert by then.'

'You will,' Kent said.

'Okay, so what's the plan once we get out to the back paddock?'

'The boys should have that mob in by the time we get out there. I want to check them over and make sure the cattle that we've brought in are in prime condition for Luke to assess.'

'They were looking good when I flew over there last week.'

'Yeah, I hope he's happy. Managing the cattle for Dwyer's is certainly worth it financially. Once you get your property set up, I'd suggest approaching them. They're great to work with.'

'I will. Times have changed, haven't they, mate?'

'They have. The days of family properties are long gone. Big business has come to the bush.' Kent shook his head.

'Since the drought ended, I reckon the country'll end up with more corporate stations than family concerns.'

'You're right, and they have the money at hand to improve everything up front.'

'But are they doing that? I'm yet to be convinced. I saw it when I was up in the Territory.' Jon changed back a gear as they reached the gate in the fence that marked the boundary of Kent's land. 'There's a lot of lip service paid to things like sustainability and reconciliation, and the employment of women but . . .'

'But?' Kent prompted.

'I might be biased, but in the past, pastoral companies typically had staff with solid hands-on experience from the ringers right up to management, even at the board level. These days, the experience just isn't there. Unless they've got a good manager, some of these holdings are going to go bust very quickly. They chase short-term profits. Anyway, I'll get off my high horse.'

'It is a worry. I know exactly what you mean. We're losing so much out here in the bush.'

'Not only the skills on the land either. As the older generation passes away, we're losing so many of the stories. The larrikinism, the bush ethos, and the old ways.'

'Yeah, old fellas like Reg. So many stories,' Kent said. 'I'm looking forward to you meeting Luke today,' Kent said. 'He's a good bloke and he knows his stuff. He came from a large family spread, went to uni and then got his helicopter licence. Dwyer's are really lucky to have him.'

'Look forward to it. What time are you expecting him? I'd like to get home as early as I can this afternoon.'

'Ryan?' Kent asked.

Jon looked sheepish as he pulled the ute over near the cattle yards 'Um, not really. Would you believe the opening of the Vintage Tea Room? Fallon said she won't go unless I do too.'

'I'm in the bad books with Sophie because I'm working too,' Kent said.

CHAPTER 3

Sophie

By nine o'clock, Sophie had six dozen jam drops, three dozen Anzac biscuits, and two dozen Melting Moments cooling on the kitchen bench. She went into their bedroom, wondering what would be suitable to wear today. She'd offered to help out in the kitchen, but she still needed to look the "vintage" part. Jenna had already worked herself up into a right state when Sophie left yesterday, and Sophie didn't want to give her anything else to worry about. So dress the part, she would.

'What if we haven't got enough food? What if nobody comes to the opening?' Jenna said.

Sophie laughed. 'Well, I think you're going to hit that magic middle spot. You won't run out of food, and you'll have enough people to eat it.

The whole town's talking about the opening, you know. Actually, the whole region. Plus look how much food you've got. We've got four Victoria sponges ready to be filled, and the biscuit jars are full.'

Jenna had nodded. 'I'm going to make some more tonight, plus a tray of vanilla slices. I'll fill the sponges in the morning so they're not soggy. We've also got eight different slices, and Jenny Riley has offered to make me two dozen plain scones and a dozen pumpkin scones. Oh, and Mrs Rees sent in three jars of lemon whisky marmalade for the scones.' Jenna had put a hand over her mouth. 'Oh, no. Maybe we've got *too* much food. Being a Saturday, everyone might be busy.'

Sophie smiled as she calmed Jenna. 'How long have you been in town?' Sophie asked.

'For three and a half months.'

'And you've made a huge hit in the

community,' Sophie said. 'Everyone loves you. Not only will you have all the tourists going up and down the highway calling in, but I think half the town is going to be out here every day for their morning cuppa.'

'It has been good this week. It was a good practice week. But I don't know.' Jenna chewed on her lip. 'I don't think that volume will be sustainable, you know. I think our main clientele will be the tourists. It's just a novelty for the townsfolk to come out and see what's happening.'

'No.' Sophie shook her head. 'You've injected enthusiasm into the community, and when Jenny Riley was here yesterday, she said because of the extra tourists that are stopping out here and with all the brochures you've been handing out, already more caravans are stopping overnight in town. I think that we'll see a lot more people doing that. And Jenny is talking about opening her gift shop again. She closed it up before I went away about four years ago, but she still owns the premises. Her Calico Cottage was a hit before COVID, but hopefully, if she opens it again, that will be another business for tourists to visit.'

'That would be great.' Jenna looked more hopeful.

'Jenna, I think you are responsible for getting Augathella well and truly back on the tourist map.'

Jenna smiled. 'Really? As long as the gala opening goes well tomorrow, I'm happy.'

'And your mum's still going be here for it?' Sophie asked.

'Yes, that's why I made it two o'clock and afternoon tea instead of morning tea. Not only will all the Saturday sports be over, but it will give Mum and Dad time to get here. They're staying at the pink pub at Dulacca tonight, and they said they will be here by noon, so it'll just give them time to get the van set up, have a shower, and get dolled up.'

Dolled up, Sophie thought now as she stood in front of her wardrobe looking at the clothes hanging in front of her.

Nothing in her wardrobe suited the vintage line. There weren't many dresses there; most of the hangers held jeans and T-shirts. There was a bridesmaid dress she'd worn when she was a bridesmaid for one of her school friends, and she still had her white dress from the Debutante Ball when she was eighteen. It should still fit, but it wasn't the right style.

Sophie frowned and reached to the back of the wardrobe, where there was a green velvet skirt she'd bought years ago for a fancy dress party. She pulled it out and slipped it over her hips. It almost fitted, but thanks to Jenna's cooking, it was snug over her tummy. She needed a loose top over the waist. A T-shirt wouldn't do.

Kent's mother, Rhonda, had left quite a few of her clothes here when they moved to Brisbane, and Sophie remembered a cream top that she had worn every time Jenny Riley had one of her spring garden parties. She walked down the long hallway to the master bedroom that was still Kent's parents' room.

Since Kent's dad had been sick, they didn't get home to Lara Waters very often. They'd moved to Brisbane before the wedding so that his dad was close to the specialist.

Sophie was sure Kent's mum wouldn't mind her borrowing a blouse. As she opened the wardrobe, she wrinkled her nose as the cloying smell of camphor drifted out.

Her eyes scanned the rows of blouses, and finally, they settled on the cream cotton blouse that she was looking for. Pulling out the padded hanger that her mother-in-law had all her clothes on, Sophie walked to the mirror and held the cream top up in front of her. It was a loose waist-length style with a scooped, gathered neck and puffed sleeves.

It would be perfect. She sniffed it carefully; the camphor aroma wasn't too bad. She could air it for an hour or so, and a splash of perfume would cover the smell of mothballs.

She carried the blouse back to their bedroom at the other end of the house and hung it up on the shower rail in the ensuite. She turned the hot water on in the bath to let the room steam up to freshen the shirt and hopefully take out the few wrinkles.

Sophie hurried back to the kitchen, took the final batch of biscuits out of the oven, and put them on the benchtop with the others. Before she went back to the bathroom to turn the water off, a quick call to her mother-in-law was in order.

CHAPTER 4

Jenna's Vintage Tea Room

Matilda Highway tourist route

Jenna Wilson smiled as she stood beside the antique Welsh dresser that she had found for her newly-opened business, the Vintage Tea Room, and watched her grandfather deep in conversation with an older man in the car park outside.

Since they'd opened last Saturday, Reg—her *newly-discovered* grandfather had asked that Jenna call him Reg—had asked for a lift out to the tearoom from town with Jenna and Alana each morning so that he could sit outside and wait for the customers to arrive.

Jenna had had no idea that the property she'd bought—for a very reasonable price—was owned by the grandfather she'd never met.

The grandfather she didn't even know she had, let alone one who lived in the town she had decided to move to. Today, her mother was arriving to meet Reg, her father, for the first time. Jenna swallowed the lump that had been in her throat ever since she'd got up at four a.m. It was going to be a very emotional day. The meeting of her mother and Mum's father, and the official opening of her new business. It was sure going to be a day to remember.

Reg gestured to the house—the house looked nothing like it had when Reg lived there—and Jenna knew that he'd be telling their first customer how he'd used to live here, and what a wonderful job his granddaughter had done, converting it into a tearoom on the highway.

Customer! Gosh, had she turned the urn on when she arrived? Alana had stayed at Kirk's place last night—that romance was hotting up quickly—and Jenna was out of their usual routine setting up by herself. It was going to be a long and busy day, so she'd told Alana not to come until ten.

Last week had been hectic and had surpassed Jenna's expectations. She was going to have to look for more staff . . . and quickly. She couldn't rely on Sophie's goodwill forever, even though she'd appreciated her help so much as the newly opened business had been flooded with customers every day.

Boy, had those customers arrived! They had only been open about fifteen minutes on their first trading day when six caravans had pulled up and a dozen people had spilled out of the cars, looking delighted they could get a cup of tea.

Reg had been there that day and had thoroughly enjoyed talking to the travellers.

'Good to meet some new people, love,' he said. 'It was pretty much always the same ones who used to come into the pub. We did get a few tourists there, but it was the good old regulars who used to keep me busy talking.'

Jenna had hidden a grin at that. Now that the emotion of discovering her grandfather had passed, they were settling into a comfortable relationship, and she was quickly learning that "Old Reg", as the town referred to him, sure enjoyed a yarn.

The phone conversation she'd had with Mum when she discovered that Reg was her long-lost grandfather and her mother's unknown father had been a difficult one.

Mum and Dad had been in Exmouth, Western Australia, and had immediately hightailed it across the country to Augathella.

Heading back to the east, their journey had been interrupted by floods along the road from Broome to Kununurra. They had stayed in touch by phone as the journey progressed, but Mum had refused point-blank to speak to Reg.

'The first time I speak to him, I want it to be face-to-face,' her mother's voice was teary. 'Don't tell him you've told me, will you, love? I want to see his face.'

Jenna questioned the wisdom of that. 'I'm surprised he hasn't asked, Mum, but I haven't mentioned you at all yet. He just asked once where you were, and he hasn't mentioned you since.' Jenna understood her grandfather's hesitation; it was hard enough for him to get used to having a granddaughter in town, let alone thinking about the daughter he hadn't known he had. 'But he does know you're on the way. For one thing, we don't want him to get a shock, and it will also give him time to prepare if he knows you're coming.'

'Okay, darling. I'll leave it up to you.'

'It will all be fine, trust me,' Jenna had promised. Now two weeks later, her parents had got through the flood water and last night had spent the night four hundred kilometres away, ready to arrive in time for the official opening.

Jenna hurried inside while Reg was still talking to their first customers for the day, and was pleased to see she *had* turned the urn on, as well as the coffee machine. She set a tray with cups and an assortment of biscuits and cupcakes, hoping that the early arrivals weren't expecting a breakfast menu.

CHAPTER 5

Sophie

Sophie dialled the Brisbane number and waited for Kent's mum, Rhonda, to pick up. She wouldn't feel right just taking her clothes and wearing them without checking first.

The phone picked up quickly, and Rhonda's happy voice greeted her. 'Hello, is that Sophie or Kent?'

'Hi, Mum, it's me, Sophie. Kent's gone out to work already.' Rhonda had insisted that Sophie call them Mum and Dad as soon as they got married. As she and Braden had lost both their parents a few years ago, it was bittersweet.

'I thought he might be. It's so lovely to hear from you, love. How are you both?'

'We are good. How's . . . um'——even though Mr Mason insisted she call him Dad, it was hard to do that—'how are you both?'

There was a long silence for a moment until her mother-in-law spoke.

'Dad hasn't had a good week, but he's a bit better this morning. So, yes, we're fine. We're looking after each other. We were hoping that you and Kent would come down to Brisbane and visit because I don't think we're going to be able to get back home for a while.' Her voice was slow, and Sophie read between the lines. Kent's dad was obviously not well.

'Yes, Kent and I were only talking about that the other day. We'll come down for a weekend soon.'

'How soon would that be, Sophie? As soon as the mustering is finished?'

'It's almost done, I think they'll be finished in the next couple of days.'

'Dad's keen to hear about this new setup with Ronnie Stuart's property.'

'I'll talk to Kent and we'll get down very soon. I promise.'

'Thanks, Sophie. You're a good girl. It's so good to have Jacinta and Ryder close by now when I need a break, but I—we—miss you and Kent too. Now I've been rabbiting on too much, it's early for you to be ringing, can I help you with anything?'

'Actually, yes.' Sophie glanced at the clock and crossed to her chest of drawers. She tucked the phone between her ear and shoulder as she pulled out her underwear to take into the bathroom. 'I think I told you about Jenna? The new arrival in town. The one who bought Old Reg's house on the highway.'

'You did. She's opened a tearoom for the tourists you said. How's it going?'

'Well, it's been open for a week, and the town has been supportive. It's certainly filled a need locally. The tourists have been stopping in their dozens too. I was talking yesterday to Rory, the builder, and Jenna's going to have to extend the car park to accommodate all the caravans that have been stopping already.'

'That's fabulous news. One day, I'll get out there and see it.' Rhonda's voice was soft.

'That would be lovely,' Sophie said. 'But what I'm ringing about, I've got to dress up for the grand opening this afternoon, sort of vintage style, and you know what my wardrobe's like. I found an old green velvet skirt that I had, but I didn't have a shirt. So, I hope you don't mind. I went down and had a look in your wardrobe because I remembered that cream top with the puffed sleeves you used to wear to the garden parties that Jenny Riley had when I was in high school. I found it in your wardrobe.'

'Yes, that's not a problem at all, sweetheart. Not only wear it but keep it. I doubt whether I'll be wearing puffed sleeves these days and low necklines with my wrinkled chook neck.'

'Don't be silly, Mum, you're still gorgeous.'

'And you're a gorgeous daughter-in-law to say that. I have to go. I can hear Dad calling. Say hello to Kent. Give him my love, and a big kiss and hug from his mum, and I hope the opening goes really well today. Send me a photo when you're dressed up.'

'I will.'

It was only when Sophie got in the shower that she remembered she hadn't told her mother-in-law about Reg being Jenna's grandfather.

CHAPTER 6

Jenna's Vintage Tea Room

Matilda Highway tourist route

The first week of the Vintage Tea Room operating at Road Mailbox 182 on the Matilda Highway, five kilometres from the town of Augathella, had been amazing. Jenna had been overwhelmed by the response of both locals and tourists. What she had entered in her business plan to earn in a month, the tea shop had taken in the first two days, and that had meant a quick rethink of food orders, baking, seating and numerous other organisational things.

Word had spread quickly, and locals had come from Tambo in the north and Charleville in the south for a stickybeak and a cup of tea.

Reg had shaken his head after three days. 'It's good for you, love—' he'd said to Jenna, '—

but when it's all said and done, it's only a cuppa tea.'

'Everyone who's stopped by has said how wonderful it was that there was somewhere on the highway to stop for a break that wasn't a petrol roadhouse.' Jenna nodded, enjoying the warm feeling that filled her when her grandfather called her "love". 'I was pleased to see that many of the caravans turned into town after they had a cup of tea here too. I think what we've done already with our local knick-knacks and brochures has fired an interest in the local area.'

Jenna had worried about taking business away from the establishments in town, but the owners of the small coffee shop up from the butcher's and the small cafe down from the pub had both called in through the week and offered her their best wishes.

'There's plenty of room for all of us,' the owner of the coffee shop had said. 'We've already seen more tourists in town this week,' the café owner had assured her.

Augathella was a lovely town with a supportive community, and Jenna was getting to know many of the locals. She'd been invited out to dinner at the pub to join a group of local young people, and the Cartwrights had invited her out to dinner at their station last week. Their new twins were the cutest babies and had actually made Jenna feel clucky for the first time ever.

When she'd mentioned that to Callie, Callie had smiled. 'You never know what will happen out here. If anyone had told me a year or so ago that I'd be married, and have three stepsons and now baby twins, I would have told them they had rocks in their heads. And now look at me.' The way Callie had looked at the babies in the double pram with such love had just about melted Jenna's heart.

Callie had told her about the on-air incident

that had led to her fleeing Brisbane and had filled her in on who was related to who in the district.

Jenna was gradually picking up the family connections, which families were related, and who ran what businesses in town. But the best thing she'd encountered was the support and enthusiasm that everyone had shown for her new business. Half the day—when her feet weren't aching—Jenna felt as though she was walking on air.

Alana—her friend who'd come west with her from the Gold Coast to help set up the business—hadn't been as social as Jenna. She hadn't taken up many of the invitations because she and her new boyfriend, Kirk, were getting pretty hot and heavy.

Jenna smiled again; it was all she seemed to be doing lately. She hadn't been this happy for such a long time, and on top of that, the joy of finding her grandfather—well, words simply couldn't describe the happiness that had brought. She was just impatient for Mum to arrive and discover the same happiness.

But there was work to be done to prepare for the day. Hopefully, Sophie would be here soon to help her get her head around what needed to be done. Alana would be here soon too, but her head was in the clouds in the throes of love, and it was hard enough for her to get the tea and coffee orders right at the moment.

CHAPTER 7

Sophie

Sophie turned onto the Matilda Highway and crunched the gears as she changed back when a road train approached from the north. She waited, wondering whether to turn or wait.

Common sense prevailed and she eased off onto the side of the highway and closed her eyes as she waited for the huge vehicle to approach. Disappointment had impacted her mood as she'd driven in but she wasn't going to let it affect her safety. She waited until the road train had passed her car, and wrinkled her nose at the smell; even though she should be well used to the smell of cattle—it had always bothered her—but today, more than usual. She swallowed as nausea threatened.

It was so cruel to see the beasts all crammed

into the two levels of the road train.

Braden always laughed at her, but Kent had tried to reason with her. 'You're a country girl, Soph. That's what we do. We raise cattle for market.'

She sighed. 'I know, it's just a soft part of me. Poor things. We look after them, feed them and fatten them and then...'

Even though Kent had hugged her and promised to try to come to the opening this afternoon, she'd detected the impatience in his voice when he'd thought she was trying to put the guilts on him; Sophie was sure Kent believed she didn't care about the property enough.

It was unusual for her new husband to be like that, but she was a bit cross too. She'd been so looking forward to the opening and she would have loved Kent to be here with her. It had been such a busy time getting ready as she'd worked with Jenna and Alana. They'd worked hard and the Vintage Tea Room looked absolutely divine. Jenna had sourced so much memorabilia, and the outfits she and Alana had bought at a vintage store in Brisbane before they'd headed west were fabulous.

And Kent wasn't going to see any of it. Her temper simmered and she tried to get over it, but the niggling annoyance remained.

Maybe it was hormonal. Or maybe it was her age—she was heading for her mid-twenties. Maybe it was seeing Callie with the new babies, but something deep inside told Sophie that she wasn't ready to be a mother yet. What she worried about most was if she'd ever be ready to be a mother.

CHAPTER 8

Sophie

The road train passed and Sophie's eyes widened as she approached the turnoff to Augathella and looked at the newly renovated house sitting on the crest of the hill. Not in a million years would you ever guess that the Vintage Tea Room business was the dilapidated house that Old Reg had lived in until a few months ago. Every time Sophie saw the house, she still couldn't believe the difference the builders had made.

They'd left most of the original rustic timber, replacing the rotten boards and Kirk, the handyman who had taken up with Alana, Jenna's friend, had done an amazing job of sanding it back and touching up the new planks to match the existing weathered timber. Rory, a builder from Charleville had done the structural work, replacing the veranda floors and the windows. He was the one who'd found the vintage front door with the stained-glass panels on a demolition site.

The roof had been fixed and painted a brilliant red that contrasted with the deep blue outback sky. Kirk had built a new set of front steps, and now as Sophie parked away from the house to leave room for the customers' cars and caravans, her bad mood finally lifted and she smiled as she climbed out of her car. Reg was in the car park, cigarette in hand, but dressed to the nines and showing an early customer where to park his van.

Sophie threw a cheery good morning in his direction before she hurried around the side of the house and put two of the baskets with her baking on the bottom step. She hurried back to the car and took out the other two. She stopped to have a quick chat with Reg on her way past.

'Morning, Reg, sorry I couldn't stop before. I've got to get this baking inside to Jenna.'

'You're a good girl, Sophie, helping my Jenna out.'

'Anything we can do to help; she's doing a great job. Last week was incredible, wasn't it?'

'Sure was,' Reg said. 'More people called in here than I've seen at the pub in the last ten years.'

'You must be very proud.'

'Proud's not the only word. I'm blessed. Never thought I'd have a granddaughter in my old age.'

'And a daughter,' Sophie said quietly. 'I believe she's arriving today. Is that why you're all dressed up, Reg? Braden said you'd been shopping.'

Reg was wearing a new pair of trousers, a white shirt, and a nice jacket, not quite a suit, but he was more dressed up than his usual navy blue work clothes.

'Not every day a man meets his daughter,' he said, his voice husky.

'Are you nervous?' Sophie asked.

He cleared his throat. 'If I tell the truth, I am. Very nervous. I mean, who'd want to meet an old reprobate like me and find out he's your father? I feel sorry for the girl.'

'Reg, you're a good man. Don't be silly. And you know we all love you, and I'm sure your daughter will too.'

He grunted and lifted the cigarette to his lips.

'One thing I'd suggest,' Sophie said. 'Maybe it's time to put the cigarette out. Not a good look for the customers.'

'Just nerves, love, just my nerves.' He stubbed out the cigarette, dropped the stub in the garden and used his boot to cover it up. 'When I'm ready for another smoke, I'll go around the back near the dunny.'

Sophie chuckled. 'Okay, I'll get these biscuits upstairs. Get some courage up, Reg. Be prepared.'

'I am, lass. I am.'

Sophie walked up the back steps, carrying the first load of jam drops. She'd come back for the others after these were upstairs.

Jenna was in the kitchen when she opened the back door; the tables were covered with plates of cupcakes and biscuits.

'Morning, Jenna.' Sophie smiled when she spotted the tray of vanilla slices ready to go into the fridge. One of those would have Kirk's name on it shortly. Jenna was leaning over the oven, and her cheeks were flushed. She stepped back and wiped her hand over the perspiration trickling down her cheek.

'Okay, Miss Vintage Tea Room—' Sophie said with a grin— 'get yourself away from that oven and get out there and greet your first customers of the day. I'll take over whatever you're watching.'

'Morning, Sophie. Thank you, but I need to watch these biscuits. I burnt the first batch.'

'Do you really need to bake more biscuits?' Sophie gestured to the table. 'I've got four baskets for you.'

'Oh, you are a pet! Thank you. I just want it to be perfect. I can barely think straight because Mum just rang. They left Charleville an hour ago.'

'So, they'll be here soon,' Sophie said.

'Yes. I told Reg. He's waiting for them out the front, and I worry about them meeting him without me out there with him.'

'He is in the car park, and he's nervous too. He could do with you beside him. I think you should be there when they arrive. It's not every day that Reg meets his daughter for the first time.'

'I know, Sophie.' Tears welled in Jenna's eyes. 'Whoever would have known that me finding this house on the Internet, and then buying it, would lead to me finding my grandfather and Mum's dad!'

'It was meant to be, Jenna.'

'It's so unexpected and so special. Mum is beside herself. She could barely keep her voice steady on the phone. Reg is excited too, and I see he's got new clothes.'

'Yeah, Braden had to go to Charleville a couple of days ago, and he took Reg down with him.'

'You don't think he's a bit over the top?' Jenna asked.

'I think he looks pretty swish, and if that's what he chose, let's tell him how good he looks.'

'He does actually. I think he's put a bit of weight on too. Do you, Sophie?'

'I do. We all have with your cakes!'

'He's not living on beer anymore,' Jenna said. 'He has so many cups of tea when he spends a day here. And he does love his cake.' Her smile was affectionate. 'Although he is keen to get back to town to the pub for half an hour on his way home to have his one beer for the day.'

'He seems really happy. I've never seen Reg so animated. He's always been up for a chat and interested in what's going on, but he's got a new spark in him.'

Jenna turned around and Sophie reached over and brushed a dab of flour from her cheek before she enfolded her friend in a quick hug. 'Congratulations on the opening of your tea rooms, Jenna. You've done a wonderful job. You should be very proud.'

'I couldn't have done it without your help, Sophie.'

'My pleasure. Now, I'll stay in here in the

kitchen once I get the last biscuits up here. You tell me what needs to be done and then go out and wait with Reg. Go to the bathroom, and put some cool water on your face. I'll look after the customers.'

'How's my hair?' Jenna asked as she reached up and patted the 1940s style that she had rolled her hair into that morning.

'You look gorgeous, but put a bit more of that red lippy on. Did you know the mayor's coming?'

'I know. Unbelievable! Listen, those biscuits have to come out in three minutes and then leave them two minutes before you take them off the tray. Put them on that cooling rack on the sink there.'

'Anything else, boss?' Sophie grinned.

'No. The tables are ready, and the coffee machine's on. Alana will be here soon, plus the four girls from the high school who are going to waitress for us this afternoon. Can you show them what to do when they get here? Amelia said she'd help too, if we wanted. Oh my God, Sophie, I am so nervous I feel sick.'

'I can show them. It will all be fine. Now go, or your parents will arrive before you're out there.'

Sophie smiled as Jenna hurried towards the bathroom. It was a wonderful day for her friend. She walked out of the kitchen to the tea room and crossed to the window; the first customers were halfway up the steps.

She looked out; there was no sign of Reg. A motorhome drove in and parked close to the gate. A door slammed, and a woman jumped out and hurried up the steps. Sophie knew straight away who it was as soon as she stepped onto the veranda. She quickly seated the first customers who were waiting at the counter.

'I'll be back to take your order in a moment.'

'No rush, love. Take your time.'

Sophie raced into the kitchen, took the biscuits from the oven, and then hurried back to the tea room. The new arrival was standing in the doorway looking around.

'Good morning,' Sophie said. 'I'm guessing you must be Jenna's mum. You could be her twin sister.'

The woman raised a shaking hand to her face. 'Yes, I'm Jenna's mum. I hope she doesn't mind us getting here too early. I wanted to get here as soon as we could.'

There was no sign of Jenna, but Reg walked up the steps and stood on the veranda.

Jenna's mum gasped and left Sophie and hurried to the door. Sophie picked up the order pad and crossed to the table near the door where the couple were waiting to order.

'Have you decided what you would like?' she asked, keeping one eye on the couple on the

60

veranda. As the two of them stood there, she looked down at the motorhome in the car park; Jenna's dad was also giving them privacy as father and daughter met for the first time.

As she took the order, she missed Jenna's exit from the bathroom, but a soft cry had her looking up. Jenna stood at the door, tears rolling down her cheeks.

No words had been spoken, but on the veranda, Reg held his arms out, and Jenna's mum stepped into them. She was crying, and a tear rolled down Reg's cheek as he looked over at Jenna. He patted his daughter's back awkwardly.

Jenna waited a moment and then went out to the veranda. The three of them were in tears as they hugged.

Sophie had always considered herself quite hard-boiled. She'd never been one for emotion, and the months living with Jock Evans had beaten out any softness that she ever had. Having the boys had helped her soften her attitude a little. She had enjoyed the nighttime cuddles with Rory, Nigel, and Petie when Braden hadn't been able to deal with them after Julia's death. Being with Kent had opened her up even more, and her emotions had softened, but she still rarely cried.

Sophie sniffed as she went back into the kitchen, reached into her pocket for a tissue and dabbed at her eyes. She filled the plates with the food order and then went back out to the counter to make the pot of tea on the order. Once she'd put the pot, the cups, and a jug of milk on the table, she smiled at the couple.

'Enjoy,' she said softly before she walked slowly to the front door and looked outside. Two caravans and a motorhome had parked in the car park, and three more couples were heading towards the house. Alana and Kirk were walking towards the back door.

Jenna and her mum were standing next to Reg. He was still dabbing at his eyes with his white handkerchief. Jenna was chattering away, and her mother was looking at Reg as if she couldn't believe what she was seeing. As Sophie watched, Reg reached out and took his daughter's hand and raised it to his lips.

Tears welled in Sophie's eyes again. God, what was wrong with her?

She leaned around the door and caught Jenna's eye. 'Jenna, there's some more customers coming up. Alana and Kirk have just arrived too.'

'We'll go back downstairs,' Jenna's mum said. 'Reg can meet your dad.'

Jenna nodded. 'Before you go down, Mum, this is Sophie. I couldn't have got everything done without her and Alana. Sophie, this is my mum, Margaret.'

The woman, who was a dead ringer for

Jenna, turned around and held out her hand to Sophie, taking one of her hands in both of hers. Her skin was soft and a faint sweet fragrance drifted over to Sophie. 'I've heard lots about you, Sophie. Thank you so much for helping Jenna.' She gave a small smile and glanced across at Reg as the customers reached the top of the stairs. 'I hope we didn't throw a spanner in the works, but I couldn't stand to get here any later, so we drove right through the night and stopped for a sleep about three o'clock this morning.'

'Well, Mum,' Jenna said. 'I think you and Dad will be in dire need of a cup of tea. I need to give Dad a hug too. Take Reg downstairs to meet him and then I'll set up a table for you all.'

Reg's chest puffed out with pride as he crooked his arm for his daughter to put her hand through. Jenna and Sophie looked at each other and smiled as they went down the steps.

'A pretty special day for Reg and your

mum,' Sophie said.

'He was pretty nervous,' Jenna said. 'He said he was just about to go around the back for another cigarette when they pulled up.'

Sophie nodded. 'It's certainly been an emotional start to the day, hasn't it? Anyway, I've got customers to look after. You go down and see your dad.'

Jenna wiped her eyes. 'It's certainly been an emotional start. It's not every day that your mum meets her dad, her daughter opens her new business, plus she gets to meet half the district where her father grew up, and where her mother and father met all those years ago. I need to pull myself together. We have a big day ahead.'

'We do. I'll get to work,' Sophie said.

CHAPTER 9

Sophie

Sophie was in the kitchen when Alana and Kirk came in the back door. 'Hi, Alana. Hi Kirk. It's a great day for the opening, isn't it?'

'Sure is,' Kirk said. 'I've come along to help, so give me a job, Sophie.'

'Hi Sophie, you look absolutely gorgeous.' Alana's gaze went from the top of Sophie's hair to her toes. 'Even your shoes are vintage.'

Sophie smiled. She'd found the black lace-up ballet shoes in the bottom of her shoe box. She'd forgotten she had them from the ballet stage she went through in her early teens.

'Not only do they look vintage, but they are super comfortable,' she replied.

'So,' Alana said. 'We didn't like to interrupt Jenna and her mum downstairs. It looks like the meeting has gone well; they're all smiling and chatting.'

'I think we're going be pretty busy. I've noticed a few vans pull up in the last couple of minutes. Kirk, seeing it's such a lovely day, you could get some more of the tables and chairs out of the shed and put them around.'

'Right, I'm on it,' he said and headed out the back door.

'He is such a great guy, isn't he?' Alana said dreamily, smoothing her hand down her floral dress; it had a sweetheart neckline and was cinched in at the waist.

'You look lovely too, Alana. Love your dress.'

'Thank you. I hope we weren't too late getting here, but Jenna insisted that we come in late because Kirk and I worked pretty late last night.'

'No, it's fine. We're all organised. I've got a

mix of biscuits already on plates'—Sophie gestured to the benchtop— 'and I've done quite a few mixed plates, because last week, it seemed that's what the customers preferred—a mixture of sandwiches, a selection of cakes, and biscuits.'

'Yes, they did, and didn't we go through some food!' Alana reached for one of the aprons hanging on the back of the door. 'Oh look, Ben and Amelia just pulled up. They're early. I'll finish off here; you have a bit of a break. I think you've been here for a while by the look of things.'

Sophie tucked up a strand of hair that had fallen from the French roll that she'd done her hair. 'Amelia's offered to help out today too.'

Alana shook her head. 'I can't get over how you all pitch in and help. Very different to where we came from.'

Sophie was waiting at the top of the steps

when Ben and Amelia reached the veranda. Amelia reached over and hugged her, and Ben kissed her cheek.

'Hey, how's it going, Soph?' he said.

'We're pretty organised. Are you here for a cuppa?'

Amelia shook her head. 'No, I'm here to help. Ben's got to go out to a property and do a job, and I figured I might as well be here for the morning instead of sitting at home.'

'Oh, that would be great. Jenna's got some girls coming out from the high school, but an extra pair of eyes to supervise would be good. It's going to be a pretty special day because there are so many people coming from far and wide. If we stuff up, it's going to get back, and it'll affect the business.'

'We're not going to stuff up,' Amelia said after Ben had left. 'It's going to be perfect.'

'Come into the kitchen, and I'll show you

where everything goes,' Sophie said. Amelia followed her in and after a quick chat with Alana, she listened as Sophie told her what had to be done.

'Not a problem, I'll start cutting up the slices for you,' she said.

Sophie headed for the door. 'I'll go and man the coffee machine. 'Oh, Amelia, while I think of it, Kent was talking about inviting you to our place during the week.'

'Yes, Ben mentioned it this morning. Apparently, they're going up to the Tambo show next week. Are you going too? I've never been to the Tambo show.'

Sophie chuckled. 'I haven't been for a few years, but yes, I'll go. I love hearing them sing. We can travel up together.'

'That sounds good. I'll run it by Ben.'

Sophie thought about the coming week. 'How about we make it Thursday night? Does that suit you?'

'It's okay with me, and I'm sure it will be with Ben. He's keen to practise with Kent. He's actually written some new songs.'

'He's very talented,' Sophie said.

'Thursday night sounds good. Don't go to too much trouble. I'll bring the salads or make a dessert. What would you prefer?'

Sophie laughed. 'I think after being here all last week, I couldn't face a dessert. Let's just have some salads with the steak.'

'That sounds good to me. Besides, I'm watching what I eat,' Amelia said, looking down.

'Don't be silly, Amelia. You don't need to lose weight.'

Alana had gone out to the laundry and Amelia lowered her voice.

'Can you keep a secret, Sophie? I'm busting to tell you.'

'I can?' Sophie glanced down the short hall

and could hear the tap running in the laundry.

'More than okay. We were going to tell you guys when we came out for the barbecue, but I can't keep it to myself any longer. We're having a baby.' Amelia's face lit up in a huge smile.

Sophie froze and then forced a smile onto her face. How rude of her not to be happy for Amelia, and to be selfish and think that would make Kent want to push her even harder.

She reached over and hugged Amelia. 'That's fantastic news.'

'It sort of is,' Amelia said. 'Entirely unplanned. I mean, we got engaged at your wedding, but we weren't going to rush into organising our wedding, and then we were planning on having kids in a year or two. I wanted to wait until Mum and Dad and all my brothers could come down for the wedding, but that could be ten years away.' She rolled her eyes. 'But it happened. I was pregnant and had no idea. I'm almost halfway.'

'Wow, you can't even tell,' Sophie said.

'I've been watching what I eat, but I've started to pop out now.'

A strange feeling—almost a tinge of envy—shimmied through Sophie as Amelia turned sideways and pressed her loose dress flat against her front. There was definitely a baby bump there.

'Anyway, we wanted to talk to you when we come out on Thursday.' Amelia kept talking as Sophie tried to process what she was feeling. 'We're going to have a small wedding and we'd love to get your ideas on where to have it and how to do it. I've got no idea, and even though Ben's on the Shire, and he knows where everything happens, he hasn't got a clue about wedding venues. We both want to get married in the next month or two so that we can have the wedding done and dusted and focus on the baby and getting our house ready.'

Sophie's eyes widened.

'That's our other news. We've bought a house at the end of Ben's mum's street. It's on an acre and has the most beautiful rose garden. And it backs onto the paddock, so I won't feel like I'm in town.'

'Wow, you're certainly full of news this morning. Ssh, here comes Alana.'

'So how are things with you, Sophie?' Amelia crossed to the drawer and took out a wide-bladed knife to cut the slices as Alana came back in. 'You actually look a bit tired, are you okay?'

Sophie nodded and smiled. 'I'm fine. We had a late one last night. We were watching that funny soccer show on Netflix that Ben told Kent to watch.'

'Ben and I watched that series last week. It's really good, isn't it? Are you sure that's all? You seem a little bit subdued.'

'No, I'm fine,' Sophie said forcing her smile to widen. She wasn't going to share what she was worried about; if she was going to share her worry, she'd talk to her sister-in-law, but then she bit her lip. That wasn't fair; Callie had her hands full with their family.

'Well, that's good to hear,' Amelia said. 'I'll look forward to having more of a chat on Thursday night.'

Sophie moved across to the window at the front of the tea room. 'I think we're going to be busy. Oh, my goodness, how many people are in that group?'

Alana joined her at the window and counted quickly. 'Would you believe twenty-four? I hope Kirk's got those tables ready to go. I'll just grab some tablecloths and run down and cover them.'

'I'll get out and start taking orders until you come back up, then make the drinks. If Jenna thinks she should come up, can you tell her that we're fine up here? We'll call out if we need her. And look, another car just pulled up. I think it's the girls from the high school.'

'Amelia, we'll put you in charge of the girls,' Alana said. 'Tell them what to do, while I go and get the outside tables organised.'

'Okay, you and I will take the orders to start with, and then I'll make the tea and coffee,' Sophie said. 'The tables up here are numbered so the girls can take the food out.'

Alana nodded. 'I'll number the ones on the lawn too.'

'Sounds good to me.'

Alana picked up the numbers from beside the phone on the kitchen bench and headed out the back door.

'Amelia, when you've done with the slices, can you man the cash register?' Sophie asked. 'Do you know how to use that Square thing?'

'Yes, I do. I was using it at Jenny's the other day.'

'Jenny's?' Sophie asked as she headed for the tea room to greet the customers who were coming up the steps.

'She's actually starting to set up the gift shop.'

'That's fantastic. Augathella won't know what's hit it soon!'

CHAPTER 10

Kent

'Well, that was a great start,' Kent said.

'Yeah, not having to repair any of the fences was great. Luke must've organised for the contractors to come in and do it since the last time I was over here,' Jon replied.

'So, we're ahead of schedule.' Kent grinned. 'We might even get to the tea room after all.'

'We probably should go home and get changed first,' Jon said.

'If you have a café like that in the country, you have to accept the customers who have to work too,' Kent replied.

'Yeah, but not on the opening day when the mayor's there.'

'True,' Kent said. 'But we won't be there until after all the official stuff is over, so we can have a bit of a wash over at the bore before we head off.'

'I'll give Fallon a call later and tell her I'll meet her there. What time do you reckon?' Jon asked. 'And it depends on Ryan too.'

Kent frowned and screwed up his face. 'All depends on what time Luke arrives.'

'It's only just gone eleven-thirty. He should be here soon,' Jon said.

'Yep, and then he might come into town with us. I think he was planning on staying the night.'

'And then maybe we can go to the pub for a beer after the cup of tea thing,' Jon added.

'Sounds like you've got my social calendar planned for the rest of the day.' Kent chuckled.

'Blame Fallon, she's been such an organising influence on me, especially since Ryan arrived. If you're not organised with a baby, nothing gets done.'

'Half your luck, mate.'

'What's up?' Jon looked at Kent curiously. 'Sounds like you've got something on your mind.'

Kent ran his hand through his hair. 'I shouldn't say anything, but it's good to talk to a bloke. I probably should talk to Sophie about it, but we've been on eggshells a bit around each other some of the time lately.'

'Doesn't sound good.'

'Don't get me wrong. We're fine. Everything is great. Marriage is fantastic. We're settling in well together. Life's good. It's just that the few times that I've mentioned kids, she seems to clam up.'

'Early days, mate. You've only been married a few months. You're probably imagining it. You know what they say. Men are from Mars, and women are from somewhere else, or something like that. I find it hard to read Fallon a lot of the time. I just listen, and I know when not to say anything and when to just smile.'

'You're probably right, Jon. Don't say anything to Fallon, will you?'

'Not a word, mate. Secret men's business. And if you ever do need to have a chat, feel free. Not that I can set myself up as a marriage expert. Who would've ever thought a couple of years ago we'd all be settled into marriage now? Callie showed up and then Braden remarried and his three boys are doing so well. The twins arrived and Callie's settled right in. Fallon flew in, and look what happened there. And Sophie came home and you pair got yourselves sorted and hitched.'

'Yeah, just ignore me. I'm making something out of nothing,' Kent said. 'But you're right. Life's good, hey?'

'Sure is.' Jon pointed to the east. 'Here comes Luke in the chopper now.'

Two hours later, Luke had checked out the

cattle, done a headcount as best he could, and announced that he was more than happy with their condition and that they were ready for the market.

Kent breathed a sigh of relief. 'That's great, mate. We can get the truck going, load 'em up, and not have to worry about letting them out in the paddocks again and then doing another muster.'

'I know,' Luke said. 'Time's precious.'

Kent leaned back and looked up at Luke, who towered over him at over six and a half feet. He shook his head. 'I wonder how you fit in that tiny little helicopter.'

Once introduced, Jon and Luke had hit it off straight away; it turned out they had a lot of acquaintances in common up in the Territory.

'I didn't know you'd worked up there in helicopters as well,' Kent commented.

Luke laughed. 'I reckon every helicopter

pilot that I've met has done some time up in the Territory.'

'Can't argue. I've never even been up there,' Kent said.

'Yeah, but you've got your family spread here, and now you're married. Plus, you've got all our stuff to look after. I can't see you getting there for a while.'

'I don't even know if I want to,' Kent said. 'It's pretty good here.'

'Right, I'll take the chopper over to your place, and I'll meet you there, will I, Kent?' Luke asked.

'How about flying into town? Land at the aerodrome in town, and we'll pick you up. There's a bit of a shindig out on the highway, and we're both calling in to keep our partners happy. You can either come with us or we can meet up at the pub afterwards. It's up to you, Luke, what do you reckon?'

'What's happening at this shindig?' Luke grinned.

'There's a new girl come to town, and she bought an old house on the highway. Belonged to Old Reg, a local identity, but you wouldn't have met him. Turns out that Jenna's his granddaughter, and she's had a whole stack of building work done at the house over the past couple of months. She's opened what she calls a "vintage" tea room on the highway. It's doing really well.'

'Anyway,' Jon interrupted. 'To cut a long story short, today is the grand opening. The mayor's come up from Charleville and there are a lot of people coming from all over the district.'

'Sophie got up at some ungodly hour this morning and baked thousands of biscuits,' Kent added.

'Sounds good to me,' Luke said. 'Might be a bit early for a beer, so a cup of tea and a homemade biscuit or two would hit the spot.'

'We've had lunch. We took a break for smoko about an hour ago. Have you eaten?' Kent asked.

'I had a bacon and egg roll at Thargomindah,' Luke said. 'I had to fuel up there on the way over.'

Jon nodded. 'You sure get around, mate.'

'Yeah, we've got properties in Narrabri, Cunnamulla, and west of Charleville. And one just over the border into the Territory and another one just past Cameron Corner. Keeps me busy getting out and looking at them,' Luke said, 'but here is my favourite stop. I know that you look after the beasts really well out here, Kent. Sure makes my job a lot easier.'

'Thanks, mate,' Kent said.

'Okay, how long will it take you guys to get into town?'

'I'll probably be about half an hour,' Kent

said.

'Rightio, pick me up at the aerodrome. On the way in I might have a bit of a fly over a couple of places I've got my eye on. The company's looking for more land out this way. Do you know of any properties that are coming up out here?'

Kent looked at Jon. Jon raised his eyebrows and nodded slightly.

'If you head southwest from here—' Jon said, '— about five ks as the crow flies, you'll see a place with a brand-new green Colourbond roof. Have a look around the eastern side of that. That's my new place. If you're seriously looking for some more land, I'm happy to take on some stock for you. I've worked as a manager at a lot of stations both here and in the Territory so I can provide references.'

'I'll suss it out on my way over,' Luke said. 'Thanks, mate.' He held out his hand to Jon and shook it. 'Good to meet you, anyway. See you in town. See ya, Kent.'

A couple of moments later, the whop whop of the chopper filled the air, and red dust swirled around them as Luke took off and headed southwest.

'Thanks for priming me on that, Kent. I probably wouldn't have said anything if you hadn't mentioned it,' Jon said. 'Luke seems like a good bloke.'

'He is. You ready to head?' Kent asked.

'Yep. Do you mind driving? As soon as we get into service, I'll give Fallon a call and see if she's got to the tea rooms yet. I'll let her know we'll be there soon. Around three o'clock, do you think?'

'Three sounds good to me,' Kent said as he climbed into the driver's side.

CHAPTER 11

Sophie

Five hours later, Sophie kept one hand in the washing-up water and reached over to wipe her left hand with the hand towel on the side of the countertop. It had been an incredibly busy day. The attendance at the gala opening had exceeded any of their expectations, and there weren't going to be any jam drops left over to freeze for the week ahead. They'd been through so many of the cups and saucers it was quicker to hand wash, dry, and put them back out on the benchtop for Alana to take back out than to run the dishwasher, even on the thirty-minute cycle.

Perspiration trickled down the side of Sophie's face, and she used her shoulder to wipe it away.

'Sophie, I need you out the front,' Jenna's

voice came from behind her, and Sophie turned, wiping both hands on the towel this time.

'Not a problem. What would you like me to do?'

'If you don't mind, I'm going to take a quick break. Mum and Dad are about to go into town and park up their van. Is that okay? Then I'll come back up and you can have a *long* break. You haven't stopped all day.'

'Of course, it's okay. Alana is handling the orders, and Amelia is plating up the food as the orders come in. She's just gone downstairs to have a short break. The four girls have been fabulous.'

'We're down to the last Victoria sponge,' Jenna said, looking in the fridge.

'Go on, scat. Hang on, take your apron off and put some lippy on before you go. You've got to look the part.'

'Was the official bit okay?' Jenna asked

hesitantly. The two o'clock official opening had gone well. The shire mayor had given Jenna and the business a huge rap.

'It was great. I think the mayor sees your business as the turning of the tide for this northern part of the region.'

'I can't believe it, just after a week of trading. Do you think the numbers will be sustainable?'

Sophie nodded. 'Jen, I've lived in this district all my life, except for a couple of years away recently, and this is the best idea I've ever seen. I've seen businesses come and go. I've seen people move here and leave just as quickly, but over the last couple of years, since the drought ended, a lot of new younger people have arrived in the district. There's a lot of innovation happening with organic farming, the new date palm place, and we're getting a real unique flavour here.'

'It's been the best day.' Jenna was positively beaming.

'It has, now I'll look after the front of house. I think there are quite a few starting to leave. It's nowhere near as busy now. What time do you want to close?'

'I guess we'll just play it by ear and see how long everyone wants to stay.'

Sophie smoothed back her hair and checked her apron. It was still clean enough to go out to the front of the house. Alana had just reached the serving bench as Sophie followed Jenna out.

'Okay, Alana, I'm on it now.' Sophie picked up the order pad and pencil and hurried down the steps. The tables downstairs were still full, even though upstairs had emptied out. It was such a lovely afternoon, everyone wanted to sit in the sun. It was such a shame Kent hadn't got here; he would have had lots of locals to talk to. She reached the table at the side of the steps, and her smile widened as she saw her brother and sister-in-law sitting there.

'Hey, guys, I didn't think you were able to come. How's our little bubs?'

Braden and Callie were sitting at the table with a pram between them. Braden's proud expression as he looked down at his twins almost brought another tear to Sophie's eye.

'Perfect children,' he said proudly. 'Not a peep out of them since we got them out of the car.'

'Where are the boys?' Sophie asked.

'We dropped them into town to Ruth. She didn't want to come out here today. She came out last week and gave Jenna her nod of approval,' Callie said. 'I think the boys would have been bored here once they ate their cake. Running around the tables on a sugar high with all that good china wouldn't have been a good idea. They were playing in Ruth's garden when we left.' Callie grinned. 'Now look at this quiet pair. They've had a feed and they're sleeping quietly.'

Sophie leaned over the pram and gazed down at her new nephew and niece. It was still hard to believe that Callie had had twins. It had been totally unexpected. Sophie would never forget that afternoon.

'Black tea for you, Braden?' she asked. 'And a skinny cap, Cal?'

'Yes, please. Where's Kent?' Braden looked around.

'Couldn't make it. Luke was flying in today to check the beasts over at the Stuart place.' Sophie pushed away the ever-present disappointment as she headed back upstairs with the order. Despite her comfortable shoes her feet and lower back were starting to ache. She stretched and rubbed her back as she walked up the stairs.

CHAPTER 12

Sophie

Finally, only a few stragglers were left. Amelia had stayed in the kitchen and helped them wash up the last of the dishes before loading up the dishwasher. Braden and Callie had come up to say a quick goodbye.

'We're thinking about going to the pub for tea, Sophie,' Braden said. 'Give Kent a call to come into town.'

'Pass. I think I need an early night,' Sophie said, rubbing the nagging ache in her lower back again. 'He'll be tired too.'

'Sophie!' Braden shook his head sadly. 'Make the most of it before you have kids.'

Sophie pulled a face at her brother. 'Maybe I'd like to spend some time with Kent. We're newlyweds, remember!'

Amelia was putting the last half of the leftover sponge in the cool room that Kirk had installed at the end of the short hall behind the laundry.

Jenna walked into the kitchen as Sophie pulled out the tray from the refrigerator that held the milk and the slices.

There were three vanilla slices left—now she had an order for two—so she took the three out, put the third one on a plate, covered it with cling wrap, and put it at the back of the top shelf.

'I'll pay you for that one, Jenna.' she said. 'That's Kent's afternoon tea, or more likely tonight's dessert.'

'You will not pay me for it at all. Don't be silly.' A knowing smile tilted Jenna's lips. 'I won't be charging for his cup of tea either.' She walked over to Sophie and undid the colourful apron that was covering her cream shirt and green skirt. 'I don't think I told you this morning how fantastic you look. I was so worked up about Mum and Dad arriving.'

'Thank you,' Sophie said. 'So do you. It's been a great day.'

'And about to get even better. Hang that apron up and go stand on the front step,' Jenna said.

Sophie wrinkled her nose with curiosity. 'What do you mean? Stand on the front steps for what?'

'It's way past time you had a break. Anyway, I think it's time you sat outside at one of the tables, got a feel for the place as a customer, and had a cup of tea.'

'I don't really need one,' Sophie said, wondering what Jenna's sneaky smile meant.

'Sophie,' Jenna said. 'Outside. Now.'

'Yes, boss.'

The official opening had gone well, and the crowd was finally starting to thin. There were quite a few empty tables in the front tea room and on the veranda. The two smaller rooms were empty now and Amelia was wiping down the tables. As Sophie walked through the house, there were still several local people looking happy and chatting with friends. The last caravan had pulled out when she had been on the veranda taking the last order. She stood on the veranda looking at the tables below, and her heart jumped as she saw Jon's ute pull into the car park.

'Kent! Jon!' she called, as her husband climbed out of the driver's side. Kent looked up and grinned as she waved to him madly. 'Oh, what a sweetie. He made it.'

She watched as the back door of the twin cab ute opened and Luke climbed out. Sophie ran lightly down the steps and across to the three men. Kent held his arms out, but she stood back with her hands up. 'Cream shirt. How dirty are you?' she said, gesturing to Kent's mother's blouse.

'It's only red dust,' Kent said. He wasn't too dirty but he leaned over and kissed her without touching her.

'I'm clean, Sophie. Not like this pair,' Luke said.

'Hello, Luke, it's good to see you,' she said as he bent down to kiss her cheek.

'Good to see you too, Sophie. You're looking very "fifties".'

'Jenna asked us to dress up vintage. It's gone so well she's going to buy some clothes especially for the staff next time she is at a retro shop.'

'Jenna?' Luke queried.

'Yes, these are Jenna's vintage tea rooms. She's been in town for about three months. You probably haven't met her yet. I don't think you were here the last time we all met at the pub for dinner.'

'I hear there's a plan tonight. But how about a cuppa now?'

'Of course. I'm pleased to see you all here. Come and sit down and put your orders in. And, Kent, guess what I saved you?'

'One of Jenna's delicious vanilla slices, hopefully.'

'Sure is, and it even has passionfruit icing for you. Jenny Riley's passionfruit.'

Kent reached out and took Sophie's hand. 'I knew there was a reason I married you.'

'Careful, there's only one piece left. I can still give it to someone else,' she replied as Kent grinned at her.

'I'll just go and try to call Fallon again,' Jon said. 'I'll be back in a moment.'

As Sophie led Kent and Luke across to a vacant table at the edge of the lawn, she took notice of how pretty the place looked this afternoon. The winter sun was low in the sky as the afternoon closed in and gave a beautiful golden sheen to the house and garden. The landscapers had done a great job; yellow roses trailed over a trellis, and a bed of colourful winter annuals bordered the fence along each side of the gate.

Jenny Riley—the local with the green fingers—had come out and given them advice and gifted some rose bushes and shrubs to Jenna. Jenna had been overwhelmed.

'You guys sit here,' Sophie said, gesturing to the vacant table.

Kent was looking over at Reg where he was still sitting with his daughter and son-in-law.

'Looks like it's all gone well,' Kent said. 'Reg is beaming.'

'They've been sitting there talking since about ten o'clock this morning,' Sophie said. 'Jenna hasn't stopped smiling since her mum and dad arrived, and when she looks at Reg, she's as proud as punch. I've lost count of the cups of tea they've had. They came out a while ago to take the van into town, and they still haven't left.'

Luke looked over at the table. 'What's she proud about?'

'All this.' Sophie gestured around. 'A lot has happened in town since you were last here, Luke. Jenna arrived and started the tea rooms. Turned out that Reg from the pub is her grandfather, and today her mum met her father for the first time. Reg didn't even know he had a daughter and a granddaughter until a couple of weeks ago.'

'Readymade family,' Luke said. 'Sounds like something out of *Neighbours*.'

Sophie rolled her eyes. 'Don't tell me you watch that. Is it still on?'

'My mum used to watch it when I was a kid.' Luke grinned.

'So did I,' Sophie took the order pad from the pocket of her apron. 'I was addicted. Now what would you like for your afternoon tea?'

Kent chuckled. '*Smoko* for us.'

Sophie shook her head with a chuckle. 'No, Kent, show a bit of class. When you visit us here at the Vintage Tea Room, you have *afternoon tea*. We've brought some style to town.'

'Very well, my love. I will have a cup of strong black tea for my afternoon tea, please.'

'Luke?'

'I'll have a cup of tea too, thank you, Sophie. Can I give you a hand to carry it?'

'I'm good, but thank you,' Sophie said. 'Any preference in the food line, Luke? There's a little bit of everything left. Scones, biscuits, fruit cake, cream sponge—'

Luke looked hopeful. 'Vanilla slice?'

'Sorry, Kent gets the last one. I've been saving it for him, but I can cut it in half.'

'No, you can't.' Kent wagged his finger at her. 'That's got my name on it, that vanilla slice.'

'How about marshmallow slice?' Sophie said. 'That's one of Jenna's specialties.'

'I'll let you choose,' Luke said.

'Okay, I'll bring an assorted plate out.' She looked up as Jon walked across to them. 'Did you get on to Fallon, Jon? I thought she and Ruth would be here today.'

'She's on her way now. She was waiting for Ryan to wake up. She won't be long. Ruth's minding Braden and Callie's boys, so she won't be coming. She was out in the yard playing cowboys and Indians with them.' Jon shook his head. 'That woman has so much energy.'

'Tea or coffee for you, Jon?'

'I'll have a large flat white, thanks, Sophie.'

Kent grabbed her hand as she went to walk away. 'You look lovely, Soph. I do love the cream shirt. Is it new?'

'It's your Mum's. I called her to see if it was okay to wear it.' Sophie hesitated, and then decided not to say anything about his dad yet; it wasn't the place and there'd be time enough for that tonight. 'I promised we'd go and see them soon,' she said.

Kent knew her well enough to read between the lines, and he squeezed her hand. 'Yes, sooner than later,' he said quietly.

'Love you,' she whispered. Sophie reached up and kissed his cheek before she hurried back to the kitchen.

Amelia had finished clearing the tables in the two rooms and was back in the kitchen.

'Probably one of the last orders for the day,' Sophie said. 'Two pots of tea and a large flat white. And a plate of assorted cakes and biscuits and of course Kent's vanilla slice.' She reached for her apron and put it back on. It was a miracle the cream shirt had stayed clean. 'Jenna, come out and meet Luke. He's a regular visitor in town. He drops by in his helicopter—or that is, his company's helicopter—to suss out the cattle. He's got a really interesting job.'

'I will. Amelia, will you please make Sophie a coffee too? You take that apron back off and go and sit with them, and I'll bring it out when it's ready,' Jenna said.

'Thank you, I'll leave the apron on, I think. I don't want to spill anything on my shirt.' Sophie smoothed her hair back and quickly put some lipstick on. She ran lightly down the steps and sat beside Kent. The three men were talking cattle and she sat watching them. Kent looked tired, but the shadows under his eyes were nowhere near as dark as Jon's.

Jon looked over at her and smiled, sensing her eyes on him.

'A late night?' she asked.

'Teething,' Jon said with a nod.

Sophie wondered how Fallon coped so well with the change in her life. She'd gone from being a helicopter pilot working with the mustering to being a full-time mum. But she seemed really happy and never looked tired.

Maybe having her mum, Ruth, close by made the difference. That was one thing she and Kent wouldn't have if they ever had children. Sophie and Braden's parents had passed away about ten years ago. Kent's parents were in the city, sadly dealing with his dad's Alzheimer's disease.

Sophie thought about how she would cope with broken nights of feeds and teething. Having a tiny human being dependent on her.

She wouldn't.

The panic began to build in her chest again. She was going to have to talk to Kent about how she felt; she needed to be honest.

Pulling her thoughts away from her worry, she looked over at Luke. His eyes had widened and he was staring at the house. Sophie turned to see what he was looking at.

Jenna stood at the top of the stairs, holding a loaded tray as she scanned the garden. She smiled as she spotted them sitting at the table on the lawn.

Luke jumped to his feet. 'I'll help Jenna.'

'Do you know Jenna, Luke?' Sophie asked, curious as to why he'd stared at her so intently.

'What? Sorry, Sophie, what was that you said?'

'I asked if you already knew Jenna?'

'No, I've never seen her before, but wow, what a beautiful woman. She looks as though she's stepped straight from a movie.'

'Not *Neighbours*, Luke?' Kent said jokingly as he caught Sophie's eye and smiled.

She raised her eyebrows.

Kent leaned over as Luke hurried over to the steps to help Jenna. They watched as she smiled her thanks at him as he took the tray from her.

'Invite Jenna to dinner at the pub to finish off the day? She's sure got Luke's interest,' Kent said.

'Maybe,' Sophie said. 'All depends on what Jenna's planned with her mum and dad and Reg. Although I think they're pretty tired; they'll probably go back to the van. They might come in and have dinner later.'

'And Reg'll go to the pub for his one beer and then back to the facility for his dinner.'

'Dinner? He won't need it,' Sophie said with a smile as she looked over at Reg. 'He's still eating cake! Okay, can you give Braden a quick call and tell him we'll come? He mentioned going for dinner when they were leaving before and I said I was a bit tired, so he'll need to book a bigger table. And Jon and Fallon, and probably Luke and Jenna. And we'll ask Amelia and Ben too.' She put her hand to her mouth and covered a yawn.

Kent moved his chair closer and put his arm

around her shoulders. 'You okay, Soph?'

'It's been a big day after an early start, but I'm fine now that I've had a sit-down. It'll be good to see everyone there.' She smiled. 'And Luke and Jenna can get to know each other, plus I won't have to cook dinner.'

CHAPTER 13

Sophie

Dinner at the Augathella pub that night was a joyful affair. The celebration for the opening of the Vintage Tea Room moved to the pub, and many people came over to Jenna and congratulated her. Sophie was pleased to see that Luke had snagged the chair next to Jenna. Every time she'd looked over, they were deep in conversation, and Jenna's cheeks held a rosy flush.

Sophie had found her second wind and thoroughly enjoyed the evening. Kent raised his eyebrows when she took turns holding little Meggie and Munro while Callie and Braden enjoyed their dinner.

She closed her eyes as Meg snuggled into her, savouring that delightful, sweet baby scent.

At least she knew she could hand Meg back to Callie.

'Do you want a nurse, Kent?' Sophie asked.

'Too right I do. Pass my little niece over here.'

Sophie handed Meg over to Kent and then turned to Braden, taking Munro from him.

'It's fabulous having babysitters in the family,' her brother said. 'Now, I can enjoy my dinner and use both hands.'

Sophie smiled as Braden leaned over to Callie and kissed her cheek. Braden's happiness was complete. Ruth and her husband had joined them at the pub for dinner, and Rory, Nigel and Petie sat opposite Sophie and Kent. Her nephews were growing quickly, and Rory's conversation with Kent about the cattle agistment made her realise there was another cattleman in the making.

Nigel? She wasn't so sure about her middle

nephew, but time would tell.

And little Petie. Her youngest nephew held a special place in her heart.

Sophie watched Kent as he turned from Rory and looked down at Meggie in his arms. Yes, seeing him hold the tiny baby made her feel happy. It suited him perfectly, and as he gazed down at the baby with her long eyelashes framing her cheeks, and her sweet little rosebud mouth pursed in a cute bow, Sophie knew in her heart that they would have children one day. She had to gain her confidence; it would be cruel to deprive Kent of the chance to be a dad.

For some reason, there had been a shift in her thinking this weekend, but she still held doubt.

As they headed out to the car park after Sean called last drinks, Jenna caught up with Sophie. 'You've worked your butt off, Sophie, and I'm going to pay you for today. If you won't give me your bank details, I'll just give you cash,' Jenna said.

'No,' Sophie replied. 'That's an argument you're not going to win. It was my pleasure to be able to help, and having us volunteer gives you such a good start to your business.'

'Well, I owe you,' Jenna said.

Sophie shook her head. 'It's the country way, Jenna. It's the way we do things out here.'

Jenna hugged her. 'Thank you. You're a good friend.'

'And that's exactly right,' Sophie said. 'It's friendship. You came to town, you didn't know anybody, and I was more than happy to help. Now I'm sure you'll be hiring some more staff, and I'll get back to my normal routine. I can come Wednesday and help you. I normally go over and help Callie on Wednesday, Thursday, and Friday, but she and Braden have an appointment in Charleville at the hospital for Petie this Wednesday.'

Jenna's eyes widened. 'Little Petie, is he okay?'

'Oh yes, he's fine now. He was involved in an accident at our wedding a few months ago, and they just give him a bit of a checkup every three or four months now. He's fine.'

'He's a little cutie. Wouldn't you love to have one just like him?'

Sophie sighed, and her head spun a little. 'One day, not just yet. What about you? Do you want to have kids?'

'One day,' Jenna said. 'I've got the business to look after, a grandfather to get to know a bit better, and on top of that, I haven't met anyone I want to share my life with. Not yet, anyway.' She looked around. 'You do look like you're half-asleep on your feet though. Where's Kent?'

'He's inside talking to Luke. He's staying at the pub because his helicopter is at the aerodrome just out of town, and he's got an early start to Longreach tomorrow.' Sophie looked at Jenna and smiled. 'You and Luke seem to have hit it off tonight.' Even in the dim light of the car park, Sophie noticed Jenna's cheeks turn pink.

'Yeah, he's a nice guy, but there are a lot of nice guys like that. Guys caught up in their careers, not ready to settle down. But you were right, he does have an interesting job. I was the same on the Gold Coast with my job at the agency. Too focused to get involved with anyone. I just had the occasional dates. As we travelled across to here, we stopped at several pubs for the night and met several guys who were very friendly and wanted to get to know us better.' She grinned. 'But Alana and I were women on a mission.'

'Yes, and your mission certainly has been accomplished so far. I'll see you Wednesday,' Sophie said. 'I hope the week continues to be busy.'

'See you then.' Jenna reached out and hugged Sophie. 'I truly, truly appreciate the help that you've given me today.'

Kent and Luke came out of the pub and walked over to them.

'Thanks for a great night, all of you. I'm heading home now.' Jenna lifted her hand and started to walk away.

'Wait up, Jenna, I'll walk you home,' Luke said. 'I'll see you next time, Kent. Bye, Soph.' He reached over and kissed her cheek. 'It was great to catch up.'

'See ya, mate,' Kent said, shaking Luke's hand 'And thank you for talking to Jon. He's excited to join up.'

Sophie turned as Kent opened the door of her car for her. As they drove out of the car park she smiled. Jenna and Luke were still standing under the lamppost, deep in conversation.

'Now that would be a nice romance,' she

said. Kent glanced across at her and smiled. 'You know, love, I thought exactly the same thing. Two really nice people without partners.'

Sophie laughed. 'But two really nice people who live a long way apart.'

CHAPTER 14

Jenna

Jenna and Luke were still standing under the lamppost, deep in conversation.

Jenna looked up at Luke, but his face was in shadow, his back to the light. 'It was great to meet you tonight, Luke. I'm sure we'll see you again. Your job sounds so interesting. You must get to meet a lot of people and visit a lot of pubs.'

'Would you believe not really?' he replied. 'I'm usually on the go. It's like this in Augathella, but that's few and far between.

Jenna tipped her head to the side. 'What about at home?'

'Home is when I catch up on all the auditing and paperwork from the trips that I do. I'm not a lot of fun, you know. I'm a bit of a workaholic. But from what I saw today and you told me tonight, I sense I'm talking to someone who understands being focused. I'm really impressed with the business you've set up out here. It's been a quiet little town the eighteen months or so I've been coming out, and it certainly was buzzing this afternoon. Did you enjoy yourself?'

'I did,' she said. 'And for lots of reasons. Did you see me talking to the older guy before we came to the pub when you guys were sitting out in the garden? He left with my mum and dad; they were in the motorhome.'

'Yes, I saw him climb up at the front of the motorhome. He sat in the middle, and I had a bit of a smile to myself. He was sitting there, looking as proud as punch as they drove out. Sophie told me he was your grandfather.'

'He is. It's a long story, but a good one. We've only just found him, so today was pretty special.'

'And on the day of your business opening.'

'Yes, I was on a high when the mayor gave me a huge rap, but that didn't compare to the joy of watching my mum and her dad meeting each other for the first time.' She was surprised when her eyes welled with tears, and she blinked them away. 'A very special day,' she said quietly.

'Hey, don't cry,' Luke reached out and wiped away the tear that was hovering on one of her eyelids.

'Happy tears,' she said. A pleasant shiver ran down her back at Luke's gentle touch. They stood together for a moment before she spoke again. 'Anyway, I better get going home.'

'I'll walk you there.'

'It's okay. We just live two streets away.'

He shook his head. 'Not at night by yourself.'

'This is Augathella, Luke. It's very safe.'

'Nevertheless, a gentleman never lets a lady walk home by herself. Do you live alone?' he asked.

'I actually share an apartment, a two-bedroom apartment with my offsider, Alana, but since we've been in town, she's found herself a man, and she spends most of the time at Kirk's place, so I'm alone most of the night.'

'Okay, well, I'll definitely walk you home.' He crooked his elbow as she stepped out of the car park, and Jenna threaded her hand through. Luke was tall and strong, and she really liked him. His bare arm was warm against her fingers, and she moved a little closer. They'd had a great chat through the night, mainly about what he did and what an exciting life he led.

It wasn't far to her place. They walked straight from the pub, and she stopped outside the gate of the unit block. 'This is home.'

'It's been good getting to know you, Jenna. I had a great time at your tea room, and I really enjoyed spending time with you at dinner.' He raised his eyebrows. 'Maybe next time I come to town, we could have dinner together.'

She smiled. 'I'll look forward to that.' She reached over and put her hand on his forearm. 'Now, you fly safely, won't you? I'll be listening for the helicopter when you leave tomorrow morning.'

'Don't worry about that. I will.'

Jenna was surprised when Luke reached down, and his lips brushed her cheek.

'Sweet dreams, Jenna,' he said, before turning away and walking back up the street.

She watched until he reached the corner and smiled when he waved before he disappeared. Jenna was surprised to feel her hand shaking as she reached into her bag and took out her key and opened the door. What a nice guy Luke Elliott was.

CHAPTER 15

Sophie

As it turned out, having a couple of days at home turned out to be a blessing. Sophie and Kent both woke up in the early hours of Monday morning. Sophie's stomach was gurgling, and she just made it to the bathroom in time before she was sick. All she could taste was the chips she'd had last night at the bistro.

She was washing her hands in the ensuite when she heard Kent call out.

'Damn, me too.' He went racing down the hall to the other bathroom. Hearing him being sick didn't help Sophie's queasy stomach at all.

They were both miserable when they went back to bed and spent the rest of the night up and down to the bathrooms. Sophie had recovered by the time the sun was up, but Kent was too ill to go out to work on the station. He spent most of the morning in bed or in the bathroom.

Sophie's stomach had settled but she still felt deathly tired so she had a very easy morning. She made herself some dry toast and a cup of tea and managed to keep that down. Then, after she checked on Kent and found him sound asleep, she went into the study to catch up on some of the paperwork for the property. She looked after the accounts and was way behind because she'd been so busy with Jenna as well as helping Callie with the twins. She hadn't had much time at the computer over the last couple of weeks.

Focusing on the accounts, the numbers, and organising the bills took her attention away from her still tender tummy, and the morning passed quickly. She looked in on Kent a couple of times, and he was still sound asleep each time she peered around their door. It had been at least two or three hours since she'd last heard him go to the bathroom. She filed receipts in their filing cabinet, shut down the computer, and wandered out to the kitchen.

Sophie was still in her PJs and wondered whether she should go and have a shower before she made herself some lunch. She was actually hungry and feeling a lot better. Standing at the kitchen window, she thought back to last night as she stared out at the garden. She'd neglected that too, and with spring coming there were seedlings to put in. Rhonda had always had the garden planted out by now, and Sophie was determined to do the same.

Her stomach gave a little gurgle and she thought about what they both ate, and she wondered what had made both of them ill.

They'd both had a different meal and hers had tasted fine. The only thing that had been the same was the hot chips; she had eaten some of the chips from his meal while she'd waited for her salad to come out. Kent had a steak with pepper sauce, and he had commented the sauce had been very creamy. Sophie had a chicken salad, and it had tasted fine, but it was too much of a coincidence that they had both got sick at the same time.

She had Jenna's phone number in her contacts, so she walked out to the back porch in the late morning sun, pulled out her phone and pressed speed dial. Jenna picked up very quickly.

'Hi, Sophie, what's happening? Don't tell me you want to come in and work because I'm not going to let you.'

Sophie chuckled.

'No, I just wanted to check you're okay.'

'I'm fine, why?'

'Kent and I ate something at the pub last night, and we've both been crook all night. I just wanted to check you're okay, seeing you're by yourself.'

'I'm fine. I'm out at the tearoom now, just

sorting out and seeing how much is left in the freezer and how much baking I need to do to reopen tomorrow. I'm even thinking about opening up this afternoon. There's a bit of traffic going past, and I can handle it by myself.'

'Don't overdo it, Jenna.'

'I won't. You take care of yourselves.'

'We will. I've got to go. Kent's just surfaced.'

'Okay, I'll see you later in the week. Bye.'

Sophie looked at Kent as he shambled into the kitchen. He was still in his blue checked PJs, and his hair was tousled. His face was deathly white, and there were dark shadows under his eyes.

'Holy hell, I hope I don't ever feel like that again,' he said. 'I don't think I'll eat pepper sauce again.'

'Come and sit, and I'll make you a cup of tea. Could you handle a hot drink?'

'Just a black one, thanks. How are you?'

'I'm fine. I got up at about seven, and I haven't been sick since then. I think I'm over whatever it was.'

'It'll have to be that pepper sauce. I can still taste it,' he said. 'You didn't have any of that, did you?'

'No, I had the chicken salad,' Sophie said. 'I'll have to have a talk to Sean and just check that the cleanliness in the pub kitchen is up to scratch. He had a couple of new kitchen hands in there yesterday, but it looked okay.'

'As long as he hasn't poisoned the whole town.'

'I've called Jenna. She's okay.'

'Crumbs, Luke had the steak too, I think. I didn't notice what sauce he had. I can't give him a call. He'd be long gone by now, but then again, if he's crook, he wouldn't have left. I might call the pub after my cuppa and see if he got away on time.'

Kent managed to finish his cup of tea, and then he yawned. 'I think I'll lie down for a while, and then I'll have a shower. Do you want to come and lie down with me for a while?'

'I was just thinking about having a shower too. But I'll come and have a bit of a snooze with you.'

Sophie settled next to Kent on top of the bed and he put his arms around her. She only intended to have a short lie down, but soon he was breathing rhythmically, and her eyes fluttered closed and she was soon asleep.

Sophie opened her eyes slowly, surprised to see the shadows on the bedroom wall.

'Wake up, sleepyhead.' Kent stood beside the bed and she was pleased to see he had a nice healthy pink in his cheeks.

'Well, you look a bit better,' she said.

'I feel a lot better. How are you?'

'I feel on top of the world. I slept so well I can't believe it. I never sleep in the daytime.'

'How about we go and have a shower?' he said with a grin. 'Together?'

'How about we do,' she said, with a smile.

CHAPTER 16

Sophie

Monday

Sophie couldn't stop thinking about what Kent's reaction would be tomorrow night when Amelia and Ben came for dinner and announced their news.

'You pretend you don't know,' Amelia had asked her on the weekend. 'Ben will probably be cross if he found out that I told you, but I really wanted to share.'

'I know nothing,' Sophie had said. 'And I will act suitably surprised and delighted when you tell us on Thursday night.' She knew that Kent would be very happy for them too. As long as it didn't cause tension between them.

She pegged his work shirts on the line and headed inside, even though she'd had a lot of sleep yesterday, she'd woken up tired again this morning. At least she hadn't been upset in the stomach like she had been yesterday morning. Kent had made a full recovery and managed to eat a normal dinner last night, but she was still not feeling terribly hungry. She'd managed Weet-Bix this morning, but it hadn't sat comfortably in the stomach.

The phone rang just as Sophie was about to go out to water her vegetable garden.

'Hi, Callie, how are you? Feels like ages since we've had a good chat. We didn't get to talk to each other much at Jenna's opening or the pub, did we?'

'No, and we left early. I looked for you to say goodbye, but you were talking to Fallon and Jon. We left pretty quickly because the twins both woke together as usual,' Callie said.

'Have you all been okay?' Sophie asked.

'We were both a bit sick after dinner on Saturday

night.'

'Sort of. I've kept Nigel home from school today. He's got a bit of a queasy tummy.'

'Maybe it's a bug we've had? Poor Sean, his ears must be burning.'

'Could be. Braden was a bit sick the other night, and then Nigel threw up last night, so I've kept him home from school today. I think the kids picked something up at school. Maybe.'

'Oh well, we wouldn't have caught that because we haven't seen you guys long enough to catch anything.'

'I don't know about that. They're pretty good at sharing germs. Anyway, Nigel's okay, he's out playing on his bike now, so I think he was just pleased to have a day off. Are you and Kent okay now?'

'Yeah, we're fine. Kent's gone back out to work today, and I'm just pottering around.'

'You're not working out with Jen. I thought

you were going to work with her today.'

'No, she insisted on me taking most of the week off. I'm just helping her out so it's pretty flexible. It's just a friendship thing.'

'You're a good girl, Sophie, and I'm going to impose on your goodness. Is there any chance of you coming over and sitting with Nigel for me for a while? I've had an unexpected call into town, but don't panic, I won't leave the twins with you. I'll take them with me, but I just don't want to take Nigel into town in case he gets carsick on the way. I have to go to the bank at eleven o'clock and sign some papers with Braden.'

'You don't need to tell me what you're doing,' Sophie said. 'It's your business, Cal. I'm more than happy to come and sit with Nigel. It'll be nice to have some one-on-one time with him.'

'I know you and Nigel have got a special relationship. I think he might have been a bit of a favourite when you had them over those months you cared for them.'

'He's a little rogue, but I love them all.'

'I know you do. He is a good boy.' Callie chuckled. 'Most of the time.'

'Okay, what time is it now?' Sophie asked.

'Just after nine,' Callie said.

'What time do you want me there?'

'Whenever it suits you. I will probably need to leave here about ten-thirty. Braden took the boys to school in the work ute, and I'm going to drive in the Land Cruiser.'

'Yep, not a problem. I'll be there in half an hour.'

'Thanks, Soph. You're a champion. I'll get the twins feeding now.'

Sophie went inside, put the washing basket in the laundry and took her jeans off the ironing board. It was a little bit too cool to wear her shorts out to the farm because no doubt Nigel would have her outside playing. She pulled her jeans on and struggled to get the button done up. She'd sampled too many cakes at Jenna's over the last couple of weeks; the jeans were quite snug around her waist.

'Sensible eating from today. No more snacking on jam drops and Anzacs when I'm helping out,' she said to herself.

It didn't take long to drive across from Lara Waters to Kilcoy Station. Callie was standing on the front veranda, watching Nigel ride his bike up and down the path to the gate.

'Aunty Sophie!' he squealed as he threw the bike onto the grass and came racing over, his arms open wide.

'Hey, there how's my boy?' Sophie scooped him up and planted with kisses all over his cheek. 'Can I have a kiss back?'

'That's for girls,' Nigel said.

'It's for big boys too,' Sophie held him close

and he stayed there. 'So, give your aunty a kiss.'

'Yucky,' said Nigel, squirming in her arms. 'Go away. Mum said you came to mind me. Did she tell you I threw up in the night? It was all orange and yellow.'

Sophie put a hand on her stomach. 'That's enough, Nigel. I don't need to know the details. Hi, Callie.' As her nephew ran back to his bike, she reached over and gave her sister-in-law a hug. 'You look fantastic. How are those twins this morning?'

'They've actually been good so far today. Megan slept six hours last night, and Munro did four and a half. Mind you, they both woke up at different times, so Braden and I didn't get as much sleep as we'd hoped for.'

'Where are they?'

'They went to sleep, so I've put them in the car already.'

Sophie looked at the car parked near the

gate, the two doors on the Land Cruiser were open and Callie had her bag next to it ready to leave. 'Okay, you go into town, and I'll look after this young man.'

'I'll only be a couple of hours, so we can have a good chat when I get home. Is there anything you need in town?'

'Oh, if you're anywhere near the IGA, maybe a couple of litres of milk and a large box of Weet-Bix. Kent goes through it like it's going out of fashion.'

Callie laughed. 'That's easy. Nothing else you can think of? Chocolate biscuits?'

Sophie put her hand on her stomach. 'No, I'm putting on weight from eating too much at the tearoom!'

Callie looked at her curiously. 'You're not eating for two, are you?'

Sophie froze. 'No, Callie.' She blinked, surprised to feel tears welling up in her eyes.

'God, what's wrong with me?'

'What's wrong, Soph?'

'Everybody keeps asking me when we're going to have a baby.'

'I'm sorry,' Callie said. 'I shouldn't have said anything.'

'No, it's okay. It's just me being super-sensitive.'

'You're not ready yet, you've only been married a little while. And you've got plenty of time.'

Sophie ran a hand through her hair, reached up, and tightened her ponytail. 'I don't know if I'm ever going to be ready. That's my problem.'

Callie looked at her for a long moment before she spoke. 'You're the only one who can make that decision, and it's a decision that you and Kent will have to make yourselves. But if you want my tuppence worth, and please don't be offended, and *please* don't think I'm putting pressure on, but I know that you would be an absolutely amazing mum.'

Sophie shrugged. 'Maybe. I don't know. I feel like I haven't got the maternal gene. I mean, I know Kent really wants kids, and it would be nice if we had some boys to help him on the property. I know how much Braden loves having your three with him, but it's a lot to think about Cal. I have to get pregnant, go through nine months of being pregnant, then give birth and then the hard part starts. I would be responsible for looking after a newborn baby. I see what you're going through with the twins. I don't know if I can cope with that. I honestly don't know if I could handle it.'

'Petie wasn't very old when you had him for those eighteen months,' Callie said. 'And from all accounts, you coped with that just fine. I hope it's not that experience with the boys that's made you doubt yourself.'

'Maybe it threw me in too quickly, and it's different when they're not yours. I love being their Auntie Sophie, but . . .'

Callie hesitated. 'It sounds like I'm trying to tell you what to do, but I'm not. All I can do is tell you of my experience. I didn't know if I wanted children, but when I fell pregnant with the twins, it made an absolute quantum shift inside me. All of a sudden, I wasn't Callie Black, I wasn't Callie Cartwright. I was Braden's wife, but I was also a person who was carrying a new life inside her. Please don't think I'm trying to tell *you* how to feel. I just want to tell you how I felt. I didn't want . . . I didn't know consciously if I wanted children. I worried about it too, and I thought that three boys would be enough. But when I fell pregnant, I felt different. I felt like a totally different person. I still do. Don't get me wrong. I'm still Callie. I'm still the same Callie I was, but it's created a new dimension for me.

I've given birth to my children. I love the three boys as much as I love the twins, but the twins are little humans that I carried and gave birth to.'

Sophie smiled gently, never dreaming that she would have a conversation like this with Callie.

'That's a lovely way to describe it, Callie.'

'We'll keep talking when I get home. I don't want to pressure you, and I don't want you to feel like I am. But I want you to talk to me whenever you need to, and please talk to Kent about how you feel. Don't feel as though you've got to go along and agree with everyone's expectations. It's your lives. You let him know how you feel, and you guys can sort it out together. Will you promise me that?'

Sophie hugged Callie. 'You get to town, girl, and yes, I promise. As usual, you're full of sage advice. Love you, Cal.'

Callie's smile was gentle. 'You be a good

boy for Aunty Soph, Rory.' She walked across to the car and checked on the twins in the back before she climbed up to the driver's seat. 'Won't be long. See you soon.'

CHAPTER 17

Kent

Kent called in at Kilcoy Station on his way back from the agistment property. He hadn't had a good catch-up with Braden, and he wanted to ask him a few things about the black Angus cattle.

He was surprised to see Sophie's car parked next to Callie's Land Cruiser at the house, but he pulled into the shed where Braden's ute was parked.

'Hey, Braden, how's it going?' Kent said as he walked across the shed to where Braden had his head under the bonnet of his ute.

'Good to see you, mate. What are you up to?'

'I was just coming back from the Stuart property, and I wanted to run a couple of things by you about the drench I've been using.'

'Not a problem. Did you see Sophie's car at

the house?' Braden lifted his head.

'I did.'

'Yeah, she and Callie have been chatting out on the veranda ever since I got home at three o'clock with the boys. We'll go and have a cuppa with them in a minute. I'm trying to replace the blasted fan belt.'

'Okay, stand back,' Kent said. 'Give me the tools.' Braden might be an excellent cattleman but if there was one thing he couldn't do, it was motor vehicle repairs. Mechanical skill came naturally to Kent; he took the spanner from Braden and got to work as Braden stood back and watched.

'I wish I had your skill,' he said.

Kent nodded. 'Not hard, mate.'

Braden stared at him intently for a minute and Kent glanced over at him.

'Tell me if I'm out of line, Kent. Is everything okay with you and Sophie?'

Kent froze, looking up at his brother-in-law. 'Why do you ask?'

'I don't know, she just seems a little bit subdued.'

'We've both been sick. Did she tell you that?'

'Yeah, but you had it worse by the sound of things. Cal said that you and Sophie both had different meals.'

'Yeah, Sean poisoned me at the pub on Sunday night with the pepper sauce, I reckon. But we're okay now.' Kent turned back to the motor.

Braden looked at him long and hard. 'We're talking about my sister here, mate,' he said.

'And my *wife*.' Kent's voice was tight.

'I'm sorry,' Braden said. 'I may be overstepping the mark, but I've always worried about my little sister.'

'Okay, can we have a man-to-man?'

Braden stared at him. 'I knew there was something wrong. What is it?'

'There's nothing wrong,' Kent said. 'It's just that . . . I don't know . . . every time I talk about having kids, I know Sophie, she freezes and she won't engage in a conversation about it.'

'Maybe she's not ready. I mean, she spent eighteen months looking after my three.'

'I know.'

'She did a damn good job too,' Braden said.

'She's probably not ready.' Kent put the spanner down and wiped his hands on the rag on the side of the ute. 'I mean, we've got plenty of time. She's only twenty-five. I don't want to be one of those parents who are in their forties, and if we have boys, they won't be able to help me on the property, or if we have girls, I won't be sexist.'

'Have you talked to her about it? I'll never forget what she said to me when she brought the boys home.'

'What did she say?'

'She said "I can't do it anymore. I spent my twenty-first birthday changing Petie's nappies." I've never forgotten it. I put a huge load on my little sister when I was weak.'

'It wasn't a weakness, mate. It was a terrible tragedy.'

'It was. But now you've got me worried about Sophie.'

'I think I'm making it worse because I can't talk to her. I've got a bit of an issue,' Kent said. 'That's why I'm keen to see if we can have kids straight up.'

Braden frowned. 'What do you mean, a bit of an issue?'

'Well, do you remember that rodeo when Sophie was up in the stands with that jerk? I lost focus and came off that cranky bull.'

'Yeah, I heard about it. I wasn't there. I

know you got taken to the hospital.'

'Yeah, well, I got kicked in the nuts pretty hard. I didn't give it a thought before, but now, when we've been married six months and we're not using anything, and Sophie's not pregnant, I'm starting to worry that maybe it did some damage.'

'Well, mate,' Braden said. 'There's one way to find out, see the doc. But the first thing you have to do is talk to Sophie about this.'

'Yeah, I know. I was just hoping that I wouldn't have to share my worry and she'd be pregnant by now. You know, if she was pregnant, I'd know that everything was okay in that department.'

'Talk to her, and if Sophie isn't ready when you talk to her about it, you need to go and get yourself checked out.'

'Thanks, good advice, mate.' Kent reached up and closed the bonnet. 'Ready for that cuppa?'

'Yeah, but I could go a beer, not a cup of tea,' Braden said.

They were laughing as they walked up to the veranda together, and Kent was determined that he would talk to Sophie tonight. He followed Braden out to the veranda where his beautiful wife was waiting for him with a wide smile on her face.

His heart did a funny flip as the love he felt for Sophie filled him as it always did.

CHAPTER 18

Jenna

Friday

'Will you have a look at that?' Alana said with a giggle as Jenna placed the last tray of sponge cake slices into the fridge.

The end of the week had slowed down a bit, and the traffic and customers at the tea rooms had been manageable. She and Alana had been running it by themselves all week. Jenna had arranged for Ellie and Aimee, two of the girls from the high school to come in on Saturday, and Laura and Elisabeth, the other two on Sunday.

'Have a look at this.' Jenna turned and walked over to stand with Alana near the kitchen window.

'You see all sorts of folks, don't you?' Alana said, shaking her head.

Jenna stood on her toes to peek over Alana's head as she leaned over and rested her elbows on the empty countertop.

A huge flash caravan with all the fancy gizmos on top, and a big four-wheel drive was parked at the edge of the car park closest to the house, leaving no room for other cars to turn around.

'He's a hefty bloke. Check out his plumber's crack. Not a pretty sight.' Alana giggled.

'His what?' Jenna looked out. There was a fairly substantial man bent over at the wheel, and his jeans had slipped down at the back.

'Haven't you heard that before?'

'No' Jenna smiled. 'I can see what you mean, but why is it called a plumber's crack?'

Alana shrugged. 'I don't know. I'll Google it.' She pulled out her phone and her words were interspersed with laughter 'Here's your lesson for the day, Jenna. A plumber's crack is from the stereotypical image of a plumber being a heavyset man bent down beneath a sink with a tool belt around the waist. The position and belt tend to pull down the back of the pants, and if those pants are too tight, they can accidentally reveal the "crack" of the upper buttocks. And that dear Jenna is where the term came from.'

Jenna laughed. "I am so pleased I have you to educate me, Alana. I must have led a very sheltered life!'

Alana giggled. 'Oh look, they're coming up now. Should I tell him to pull up his jeans? If we get any of the grey nomies coming in, the older ladies will be quite scandalised.'

Jenna laughed. 'I don't think they'll be scandalised; they'll probably just turn away. Oh my God, Alana, look at the lady with him.'

A young woman of a similar size to the overweight man walked around the back of the van and bent over next to him. From the tops of her thighs down to her knees, the backs of her legs were covered with tattooed writing.

'I wonder what her tattoos say,' Alana said. 'Will I read them when she comes up? Her shorts are very short.'

'No, I think reading her legs would be a bit obvious,' Jenna said.

'Well, why would you get sentences tattooed on the backs of your legs if you didn't want people to read it?'

Two more couples followed the woman under discussion up the steps. 'Come on, back to work. You take the orders, I'll get the food and make the drinks,' Jenna said.

Alana grinned at her and walked out. Jenna missed her in the apartment. Alana had now moved in permanently with Kirk in his house down past the primary school.

'I know it's a bit quick,' she'd said when she told Jenna she was moving in with Kirk two days ago. 'I knew as soon as I met him, he was the one.'

'As long as you're happy,' Jenna said.

'I couldn't be happier, even thinking that I'll probably end up settling here in Augathella. Kirk is quite settled here.'

A few minutes later, Alana came back in with the orders for three flat whites, two cappuccinos, and a pot of tea. 'Two plates of assorted cakes please.'

'Coming right up,' Jenna said as she worked on the coffee machine.

She set the trays neatly and placed one of the roses that Jenny Riley brought in for her every afternoon, on each tray.

Alana came in and took the trays with a smile. She spoke quietly. 'Mr and Mrs. Tattoo took a while to decide, but they would like two large lattes, please, made on skim milk with only half a shot. And that's *my* please, not theirs. They are rude people. They wanted vegemite toast, but I said we only have what's on the board. He wasn't happy.'

'I'll check the freezer,' Jenna said. 'I think there's a loaf of wholemeal bread in there. But tell them we can do jam but not vegemite.'

A couple of minutes later, she put the two lattes on a tray ready for Alana to take out. Jenna frowned as the sound of raised voices reached her from the tearoom.

Alana was quickly back in and shook her head as she picked up the tray. 'No, he said he doesn't want any of that wholemeal stuff. He wants white bread.'

Jenna shook her head. 'We haven't got any until lunchtime when the delivery comes, not that it really matters as toast isn't on the menu. Would you like me to go out and tell him?'

'No, it's all right. I can handle that,' Alana said. 'There's a few more coming in. Mrs Clark is on the way in for her regular decaf if you want to start making it.'

A few more arrivals kept Alana and Jenna busy for the next half hour or so.

Jenna had finished the last order and gone back into the kitchen when Jenny Riley arrived with the roses.

'Hi, Jenny,' Jenna said. 'You're early today.'

'Yes, I'm on my way to Charleville, so I picked these for you yesterday afternoon and put them in the fridge. I'm going down to do some paperwork for my new shop.'

'Oh, that's fabulous. You're going ahead with it,' Jenna said.

'I am,' she said. 'Listen. I've had an idea. I'm only opening it a couple of days a week because I've got a school-based apprentice working in my garden with me, doing some horticulture. They've done everything they can at my place because it's established already. How would you feel about it if they came out here with me and I worked with them for a couple of weeks to get your gardens ready for spring?'

'Really?' Jenna said. 'That would be fantastic. They're already looking good thanks to your work, but if you could do some more, that would be awesome.'

'You can get your own roses going out here, and then you can pick your decorations for your trays,' Jenny said.

'That sounds wonderful. Would you like a cup of coffee before you head out to Charleville?'

'Just a quick one.'

Jenna put the roses in the cool room and then walked out to the front with Jenny where the coffee machine was near the cash register. Alana was standing over in the corner with her hands on her hips, talking to the man at the register.

'Take a seat, Jenny. I'll come back and make your coffee,' Jenna said. She walked over to the counter, and the man glared at her.

'Are you the owner of this place?' he demanded.

'I am. Is there a problem?'

'Is there a problem?' he yelled, and heads turned. 'First off, you didn't have any white toast, and second, my coffee was stone cold.'

Jenna bit her lip, tempted to say that it would be cold because it was half an hour since she'd made it.

'Not a problem, sir. I'll make you a fresh one.'

The customer is always right, she told herself.

'Don't bother,' he said, nudging his wife beside him. She put her hands on her substantial hips.

'We don't want another one because my

coffee tasted off.'

Jenna couldn't help looking down. The woman's legs were lily-white, and she wore the shortest pair of shorts that Jenna had ever seen. 'Very well. If you don't want more, that will be nine dollars and fifty cents.'

'Well then, if you insist on us paying for that shit you call coffee, make us another one.' The man clomped back to the table muttering under his breath, but his tirade was interrupted by a calm voice.

'I think you should apologise for your language, sir.'

Jenna's head flew up as several others in the tearoom nodded and voiced their agreement with the new arrival.

The plumber man had sat down again and Luke was standing beside his table. Her heart beat a little faster as he walked across to the counter.

'You handled that very well, Jenna, but I'm here to back you up if you need it.'

'It's okay. If he comes back and refuses to pay a second time I'll just ask them to leave. It's not worth the argument.'

The man stood, hitched up his jeans and scowled. 'Come on, we're leaving,' he said to his wife.

Luke and Jenna watched them leave, and then she turned to Luke. 'Good morning, Luke, you're a surprise visitor.'

'I was hoping I could talk to you about dinner at the pub tonight.'

'You'll never get a table at the pub on a Friday night,' Jenna said. 'It's always busy.'

His grin was wide. 'I called in there on my way past and booked a table, hoping that you'd say yes.'

Jenna's heart soared and she smiled. 'That sounds lovely. Are you out working today?'

'No, I'm not.'

She frowned. 'So, you just called into Augathella on your way past?'

'No, I came especially to ask you out to dinner.'

'In the helicopter?'

'No, that wouldn't be the right thing to do. I had a rostered day off today, so I drove up to see you.'

'You drove up? How long did that take?'

'It's not far. I like being in the car for a change.'

'How far?'

'About four hundred kilometres. I stopped overnight at the Nindigully Pub.'

Disbelief flooded through Jenna. 'You drove that far just to see me?'

'I did. And now that I see you, I know it was worth every minute.'

Heat ran into her cheeks, and Alana winked

at her from behind Luke.

'We don't close here until three. What are you going to do all day? Drive out to see Kent?'

'I thought you might have some odd jobs here I could fill in the day with. I believe you've got volunteers working with you. I'm happy to be one too.'

'All day? Really? On your day off?'

'Not a problem at all.' Luke rolled up his sleeves. 'Give me a job.'

'A job?' Jenna put her head to the side and her cheeks warmed as he held her gaze.

'Yes, I figured if we couldn't spend the day together—which I knew we couldn't when I headed up here—I could still spend it in your company.'

Pleasure filled her as she smiled back at him. 'Thank you, Luke. It's good to have you here. And as well as appreciating your help, I'll enjoy your company too.'

CHAPTER 19

Kent

Kent helped with wiping up and loading the dishwasher before going for a shower. When he came through to the bathroom, Sophie was already in bed with only the bedside light on.

'It was a nice night, wasn't it, Sophie?'

'Yes, it was. Amelia and Ben are a lovely couple.'

'I'm looking forward to the Tambo show. I'm pleased that you and Amelia are coming with us.'

'And Ben's written three new songs.'

'I liked the sound of the one that he sang.'

'Yes.' The unspoken issue between them was Amelia's pregnancy. Ben and Amelia told them as soon as they arrived which had created tension between Kent and Sophie all night.

Sophie had pretended to be suitably

surprised, and Kent had smiled widely as he shook Ben's hand and hugged Amelia. 'Great news, guys.'

Now they lay side-by-side in the dark, and Kent sensed that they were both lost in their thoughts.

'I hope the barbeque sausages weren't off,' Sophie said. 'I feel a bit queasy again. How about you?'

'No, I'm okay,' Kent replied.

More silence followed. Sophie closed her eyes, and a tear squeezed out from beneath her closed lids. She had seen the look on Kent's face when Amelia and Ben had announced their pregnancy, and it had broken her heart. Maybe she was going to have to reconsider. Perhaps they needed to try harder, even though she wasn't ready and they weren't using any birth control. But so far, nothing had happened.

Sophie was about to open her mouth to talk

to Kent about her feelings and her love for him when he spoke first.

'Sophie?' He rolled over and put his arms around her, holding her close. 'I need to talk to you,' he said.

She stiffened in his arms. 'What's wrong?

'Calm down, relax, it's nothing bad.'

'It's about Ben and Amelia having a baby, isn't it?' she asked, her voice trembling.

'Sort of. We haven't been talking as much about things, have we, darling?'

'No, we haven't,' Sophie admitted. 'And it's because we're both worried about things, I think. Kent, I know you want to have a baby, and I sense that you aren't sure if I'm ready.'

'I've wondered. You haven't talked much about it.'

'I'm coming around to the idea,' Sophie replied. 'When I held little Megan and Munro at the pub last Sunday night, something shifted inside me. I'll be honest; I don't know what kind of mother I'll be. I don't know if I can do it or if I'll be any good at it.'

'Sophie, you'll make a great mother,' Kent reassured her. 'You're such a loving person. But if you're not ready, we'll wait. Even if it's two years, five years, or ten years, we're both young enough. We don't have to rush. But I do want to tell you what's worrying me. If we choose not to try for a baby now, I need to go to the doctor.'

Sophie rolled over, turned on the bedside light, and propped herself up on one elbow, looking down at her husband. 'What do you mean you need to go to the doctor?'

'Well, we're not using any contraception, and we've been married for nearly six months, and nothing has happened yet. That doesn't mean there's nothing wrong,' Kent admitted. 'I occasionally experience a bit of discomfort down there, so I worry that maybe there is a problem.'

Sophie sat up and folded her arms. 'That's it, Kent Mason. You are going to see the doctor tomorrow. Not to determine if you can have children, but just to make sure that everything is okay. Remember that campaign young Jerry Munsie from school started when his older brother got testicular cancer? You, of all people, should be aware of that. He was even in your year.'

'I'm not worried about anything like that,' Kent said.

'Well, you should be,' Sophie replied. 'As soon as we wake up in the morning, we're going to make an appointment to see Dr. Harry together.'

Kent grinned and reached out, pulling Sophie down so her head was nestled on his shoulder. 'That's my Sophie,' he said. 'And listen, let's forget about babies for a while, okay? We can enjoy Maggie and Munro without any pressure.'

'No,' Sophie said, shaking her head. 'We will go and get you checked out, and then we'll just let nature take its course.'

'Wouldn't you like to let nature take its course now?' Kent asked, his lips warm against her neck.

Sophie nodded and put her arms around her husband's neck and lost herself in his kiss.

CHAPTER 20

Kent

Friday

Since Sophie had insisted on scheduling an appointment with Dr. Harry the next morning, Kent decided not to go out to the farm. They slept in, and around eight o'clock, he rolled over.

'There are plenty of tasks I can handle in the shed before Harry opens at nine. I'll get up, have a shower, and we can have breakfast together. Then I'll go and do some work in the shed.'

'No, you stay right there,' Sophie replied. 'I was just about to get up and have my shower.' He nodded and lay back on the pillow as Sophie headed for their ensuite.

The previous night, when Kent had unburdened himself to Sophie, had lightened his worry. Knowing how she felt had cleared the air between them. Afterwards, they held each other all night.

Kent smiled as Sophie emerged from the bathroom and walked over to her chest of drawers. Her strong, lithe figure, the result of her hard work around the property, was evident. Her calves were finely defined, and her figure was slim and toned. But when she turned around, Kent's eyes widened.

He stared at Sophie and then sat up. 'Sophie, where are you feeling those tummy pains?'

'It's not exactly pain, just discomfort down here,' she replied, turning the light on and standing there in her underwear and bra, pointing to her lower abdomen.

'I think you should see the doctor today too.'

'I'm feeling better now, Kent. I'm fine. I don't need to see the doctor, but I'm going there with you.'

'But your tummy is all sort of bloated.'

'No, it's not,' she said looking down.

'It looks normal from the front, but you look puffy above your panty line.' Kent pointed.

Sophie reached down and touched her tummy. 'You're right. Maybe I should go and see Dr Harry.'

Kent climbed out of bed and approached her, putting his arms around her. 'We'll be fine, sweetheart. We'll get ourselves checked out and healthy, and then maybe we'll head down to Brisbane to see Mum and Dad next weekend. What do you think?'

'I think that would be a great idea. It'd be wonderful to see Jacinta and Ryder again too. I was talking to her on the phone yesterday. She's got a job at a small primary school in the hinterland of the Sunshine Coast.'

'That's quite a commute for her, isn't it? It's not close to Mum and Dad's place.'

'It's halfway between, apparently, but she

mentioned that they are seeing a lot of your dad.'
She nodded. 'I think you're right. We should plan a visit soon.'

'We will,' Kent said. 'Anyway, my dear wife, get out there and fetch me some breakfast while I get showered.'

Sophie laughed and picked up the pillow and tossed it at him. 'You can make your own breakfast. I've already had mine.'

'You have not. You just got out of bed.' The pillow went sailing back towards Sophie. Her giggles made Kent smile.

***

'Hi, Sophie. Hi, Kent,' Laura, Dr Harry's partner and receptionist, greeted them. 'Haven't seen you guys for a while. How have you been?'

'Well,' Kent replied with a grin, 'I'd like to say we're doing great, but seeing we're here to see the doctor, that might not be the right response.'

Laura smiled. 'I didn't mean personally; you know what I mean. How have you both been? Is life treating you well?'

Kent put his arm around Sophie's shoulders. 'Life's been good, thanks, Laura. We've been keeping busy, settling into married life, and overall, we're happy.'

'That's all we can ask for,' Laura said. 'You both look well anyway.'

'That's good to hear.'

Laura continued, 'Harry is ready to see you. He came in early this morning. He'll be at the hospital at ten. Thanks for taking the early appointment.' She led them to Harry's office, knocking on the door and then holding it open for them to go in. 'Harry? Kent and Sophie Mason are here to see you.' Laura stepped back. 'Harry's ready to see you now.'

After they greeted Dr Harry, he said, 'The weather's been good, Kent. I bet that bit of rain we had a couple of nights ago was good for your property.'

'Yes,' Kent replied. 'The station is looking great. We've been keeping busy, though.'

'That's the life of a farmer, isn't it?' Dr. Harry remarked.

Sophie remained standing when Dr Harry gestured for them to sit down. 'I'll let you go first, Kent. I'll go out and talk to Laura while you talk to Dr Harry.'

'Thanks, love.' Kent looked grateful. Sophie stood up, but he was at the door before her and opened it. She reached up and touched his face. 'It's all going to be fine, sweetie. Don't worry.'

'So, Laura, what have you been up to?' Sophie asked after she'd taken a seat near the reception desk in the small surgery.

'Well, Harry and I've been away. We went back to New Zealand and visited some of my family. It was very good to catch up, and make our peace.'

'You do look happy,' Sophie said.

'I am,' Laura said simply. 'I love living in Augathella.'

'And you love living with Harry, Laura?' Sophie asked.

'I do. I could live anywhere with Harry. I think that's the main attraction of Augathella.' Laura shook her head. 'Although I'm enjoying living here. Jenny Riley and I have struck up a friendship, and I'm helping her with her garden party; it's not long away.'

Sophie said, 'No, it's not. It's going to be great. I think it will be a big event this spring. Have you been out to Jenna's new tearoom?' she asked.

'No, we only got back to town a couple of days ago. I believe the opening was very good. I think everyone has been there and has been talking about it and what a wonderful job she's done. We did notice it as we drove in. Looks fantastic.'

'Fancy Old Reg's house looking like that, and how about him already having a granddaughter and a daughter,' Sophie said.

'It's lovely, isn't it?' They chatted for a while longer and then the door opened, and Kent came out.

'Your turn,' Kent said, then smiled and added. 'All good.' He was holding a piece of paper. 'I have to go down to the hospital and have a blood test. Do you want me to do that while you go in?'

'No, wait for me,' Sophie said. 'I won't be long. I might have to have some blood tests too.'

Laura had put her head down and was typing, ignoring them to give them some privacy.

'Okay, I'll wait.' He opened the door for Sophie, and she stepped inside.

'Come on in.' Harry gestured to the seat.

'So, Sophie, how are you really? I sensed when Kent spoke to me that there might have been a couple of issues there, and that's why this has come up. If you want to talk to me about it, you know everything is confidential.'

'Thank you, Harry. I guess one of the reasons I haven't gotten pregnant is because I've been making sure I've been out of bed early around the middle of the month. I sort of don't know if I'm ready to have a baby yet, even though I know Kent wants to have one very much,' she said. 'But you know what, when I heard a friend was pregnant last week, there was sort of a bit of a change in me, and I think I might be ready now. I had a few doubts, but once Kent and I talked it over, I'm feeling better, and I guess if it happens when it happens, I'll be able to cope.'

'And why did you think you couldn't cope? "Cope" is a strange word to use.' Dr Harry sat back and waited for her answer.

'I guess having Braden's boys for those eighteen months made me realise what a responsibility it is.'

'Yes, however, three children might be a bit different to a newborn baby.'

'I know. I've been seeing Callie and Braden with the twins and how easily Callie does it. I was helping a couple of days a week, just with the washing, the cleaning, and cooking and stuff like that, but she's fine now, and she's got five children.'

'I'm sure if it's meant to be, it will happen, and you'll cope. I know that sounds like a platitude,' Harry said. 'But I'm a great believer in letting nature follow its course.'

Sophie smiled. 'That was the phrase we used yesterday morning. And last night we had a good chat. And why I'm here now is because of some tummy problems I've been having. Kent commented this morning that I was bloated and made me come with him to see you. I'm feeling better now, though.'

'Okay, hop up onto the table, and I'm going to have a little bit of feel of your tummy. Just lift your shirt, and I'll loosen your trousers.'

Sophie lay there and looked at the ceiling as Harry's warm, soft fingers gently prodded her tummy. He started above her waist and moved along the base of her ribs. 'Any pain there?' he asked.

'No, all good.'

He moved across the lower quadrants of her stomach and pressed gently. 'Any pain there?'

Sophie shook her head. 'No, I feel fine. All good, and like I said, I was only a little bit queasy yesterday, and apart from that, I'm fine. It's just what I ate.'

'Okay, I'd just like you to go into the back room here.' Harry handed her a small cup 'I'd like you to give me a sample of your urine. Now tell me about your periods first. When was your last period?'

'A couple of weeks ago.'

'Regular?'

'As clockwork. They've always just been light, maybe a little bit lighter over the last few months, but I haven't worried.'

'Have you ever been on the pill?' he asked.

'Only when I was with my previous partner,' she said reservedly.

'And how long have you been off the pill now?'

'About a year and a half.'

Harry nodded. 'Okay, leave the sample in there on the bench when you finish and come back out.'

Sophie did what he asked, and when she finished, she washed her hands and left the sample jar on the bench. She was starting to wonder what Harry was looking for. She went back outside and sat back down in the chair next to his desk. 'Will I need to have some blood tests too?'

'Yes, we'll do the whole raft of tests just to check how your general health is, but there is another test I want to do, but I'll just run one quick test while you wait. I'll be back in a moment.'

Sophie resisted looking at the computer as she waited patiently for Dr. Harry to come back out. He was only gone about five minutes, and the door opened, and she looked up as he came in. He sat on the chair beside her and looked at her for a moment before he spoke. 'So, Sophie, sometimes a woman's body follows its path in different ways.'

Her eyes narrowed. 'What are you saying, Harry?'

'Well, I'll tell you first, and then you can

decide whether you want Kent to come in.'

'Tell me what?'

'You're pregnant, Sophie.'

Sophie put a hand to her throat and stared at him. 'I'm pregnant?' she whispered.

'Yes, the urine test confirmed my suspicion. At a guess, I'd say you're at least four months pregnant.'

'What? Four months?' she said, her voice squeaking.

Harry smiled. 'Yes, four months now. Tell me, what's your immediate reaction to that? Is it shock, horror, or disappointment? I want to know how you're feeling.'

Sophie's heart was racing, and she pressed a hand to her chest as a smile broke over her face. 'I'm having Kent's baby.'

Harry chuckled. 'Well, I was assuming it's your husband's.'

Sophie laughed with Dr Harry. 'How am I

feeling? I feel incredible. I can't believe it. Is that why I was sick?'

'I'd say so. With the different symptoms between you and Kent, I'd say he was the only one with food poisoning, and you said you've been queasy on and off ever since. And there's no doubt that your pregnancy test is positive. You're pregnant, Sophie.'

Her voice shook. 'Can you ask Kent to come in, please?'

'I can.' Harry patted her shoulder as he walked to the door and opened it. Kent came back in and frowned as Sophie sat straight on the chair and composed her features.

'Sophie?'

They all sat there quietly for a moment, and Kent looked from one to the other. 'What's wrong, sweetheart? What's the matter? You look a bit pale. Harry, what did you tell her?'

'I'll let you tell him, Sophie.'

'Well, Kent, I don't think we need to worry about what you were worried about anymore.'

Kent's face screwed up in confusion. 'What do you mean? What was I worried about?'

'About your family jewels?' That brought a half-smile to Kent's face but he still looked worried.

Sophie jumped up and reached over and put her arms around his neck. 'Yes, Kent, it's all good news. We're having a baby. I'm pregnant.'

For a moment, Kent's eyes widened as shock set in. 'You're pregnant? We're pregnant? We're having a baby?' he repeated.

'We surely are, and we haven't got a long pregnancy to worry about.' Sophie's smile widened. 'In fact, I think I'm probably due the same time as Amelia. Whoops,' she said.

'It's okay,' Harry said. 'I know Amelia is pregnant, don't worry, it's not a secret.'

Kent stood and put his arms around Sophie

and rested his cheek against hers. 'How do you feel about it, babe?'

'I feel really, really happy,' she said. 'It's... it's the right thing. The right time.'

'You really mean that?'

Sophie stepped back and looked up into her husband's eyes. 'I do.'

And she did.

CHAPTER 21

Three months later

Kent's sister, Jacinta and her partner, Ryder, drove Kent's parents to Augathella for the baby shower. The look on Kent's dad's face when he stepped out of the car at the homestead that he had lived in all his life had torn at Sophie's heartstrings. Mr Mason—she had always had trouble thinking of him as Dad— had been on the new trial for the drug, Donanemab. The drug had been able to slow the progression of his symptoms of Alzheimer's disease and to Rhonda and the family's great relief, his deterioration had stabilised.

As Sophie stood in their bedroom getting ready for the combined baby shower that Jenna was hosting at the Vintage Tea Room, she could hear the laughter from the shed, interspersed with the yells of three of her four nephews. Rory, Nigel, and Petie were feeling very grownup to be allowed in the shed with the men talking cattle. Munro, the fourth nephew and his twin sister, Meggie, were in the living room in their car carriers ready to travel to the baby shower with Callie.

Kent, Ryder, and Braden were listening to Mr Mason's stories of the property in past years.

'Sophie?' Callie's voice followed the soft knock on the door. 'Are you ready for me to do your hair?'

'Come in, Cal. I'm ready.'

The door opened and Callie stepped in, looking elegant in a pair of black trousers, a glittery gold top, and dangling black and gold earrings. Jenna had insisted that everyone dress up today. The women were helping Sophie get ready, not that she needed any help slipping on her floral maternity dress and jewellery, but she loved having the house full of family.

Sophie would never forget the moment when she and Kent had sat in his parents' kitchen in Brisbane and told them, and Jacinta and Ryder that Sophie was having their baby. Everyone had cried; even Kent and his dad had shed a tear. Jacinta had let out a huge whoop and danced Kent around the kitchen.

When they had come home, they had shared the news with Braden and Callie, but it was Amelia who had been one of the happiest to hear the news because as it ensued, she and Sophie were both due on the same day.

They fully intended to keep Dr Harry and Laura, the midwife, busy. The multipurpose health service had been fighting to keep the maternity section open, and both Sophie and Amelia were on a committee working towards that solution and so far, it appeared they would be able to have their babies locally.

'You look gorgeous, Sophie,' Callie said as she approached wielding the hairbrush.

'Thank you, Cal. As gorgeous as is possible with a huge stomach and swollen ankles!'

'You keep an eye on that, won't you?'

'Kent is checking on me all the time, and Dr Harry isn't too concerned, but he's got me on weekly visits now, just so he can keep an eye on it.'

Sophie sat at the dressing table and closed her eyes as Callie put her hair up into the same sort of French roll she had worn for the gala opening of the Vintage Tea Rooms. She hadn't even known she was pregnant that day, but her aching back and legs had shown her that she should have picked the symptoms. She would know next time.

And Sophie was sure there would be a next time. Hopefully, several.

The past three months had been full of joy,

celebrating their pregnancy and their happiness, celebrating the improvement in Kent's father's condition. Watching little Meggie and Munro grow into babies that were taking notice and alert had been exciting, knowing that that was ahead for her and Kent.

'You know who I think is the most excited about you having a baby, Sophie?' Callie said.

Sophie looked up into the mirror and smiled at her sister-in-law. 'I know exactly who you're going to say. It's Petie, isn't it?'

'It is, he loves the twins, but when we told him that Aunty Soph was having a little baby he was beside himself. I think you'll have a readymade babysitter over the next few years.'

'Bless him,' Sophie said.

Footsteps pounded up the front steps. 'Are you girls ready yet?' Braden called from the front door.

There was a convoy taking them to the baby

shower. The cars were full of laughter and chat as they drove into Augathella. Callie had Rhonda and the twins in their Land Cruiser, and Ryder was driving Jacinta and Sophie. When he turned off the highway behind Callie, Jacinta's eyes widened. 'Oh, my goodness, Sophie. That can't be Reg's old place.'

Sophie nodded and smiled. 'It is. Wait until you meet Jenna. She is so lovely.'

As Ryder parked the car and Sophie waited for him to come around to the back seat and help her down, Sophie admired the Vintage Tea Room.

Reg's derelict house had once been a faded building of rotten timber, surrounded by dead brown grass and old car bodies.

Now in the final month of spring, the grounds looked superb. Jenny Riley had been hard at work preparing for the Spring Garden party which was going to be held at the tearoom next week. The gardens were already in bloom with masses of colour. Somehow with Jenny's green thumb, she managed to get plants unaccustomed to the climate of the west not only adapting but thriving.

Sophie caught her breath as Ryder helped her out and she looked at the house. Whoever had helped Jenna get the tea room ready for this afternoon's function had excelled themselves. Bunches of pink, blue, and yellow balloons hung off the front of the building and coloured ribbon wound around the railings of the front steps.

Amelia and Jenna appeared on the veranda, closely followed by Alana.

'Come on, Mrs Mason,' Amelia called down. 'It's time to party.'

Sophie grinned up at the newlywed Amelia. 'I'm on my way, Mrs Riley!'

THE END

Stay posted for the births of Sophie and Amelia's babies, and the spring garden party. Will Luke Elliot come back to Augathella to woo Jenna, or is Jenna too enthralled with Amelia's brother, Josh? And what impact will Emily, the new teacher in town, have on Jenna's relationships?

Pre-orders available for An Augathella Spring:
eBook:
https://www.amazon.com.au/gp/product/B0CJL37H6L

Print: https://annieseatonstore.ecwid.com/

OTHER BOOKS from ANNIE

Whitsunday Dawn

Undara

Osprey Reef

East of Alice

Porter Sisters Series

Kakadu Sunset

Daintree

Diamond Sky

Hidden Valley

Larapinta

Kakadu Dawn

Pentecost Island Series

Pippa

Eliza

Nell

Tamsin

Evie

Cherry

Odessa

The Trouble with Jack

Healing His Heart

Sunshine Coast Boxed Set

The Richards Brothers Series

The Trouble with Paradise

Marry in Haste

Outback Sunrise

Richards Brothers Boxed Set

Bondi Beach Love Series

Beach House

Beach Music

Beach Walk

Beach Dreams

The House on the Hill

Second Chance Bay Series

Her Outback Playboy

Her Outback Protector

Her Outback Haven

Her Outback Paradise

About the Author

Annie lives in Australia, on the beautiful north coast of New South Wales. She sits in her writing chair and looks out over the tranquil Pacific Ocean.

She writes contemporary romance and loves telling stories that always have a happily ever after. She lives with her very own hero of many years and they share their home with Toby, the naughtiest dog in the universe, and Barney, the ragdoll puss, who hides when the four grandchildren come to visit.

Stay up to date with her latest releases at her website: http://www.annieseaton.net

www.ingramcontent.com/pod-product-compliance
Lightning Source LLC
Chambersburg PA
CBHW010543170726
48285CB00008B/2731